PERFECT MELODY SILENCED

BELLA AND THE BEAST MASTER

A GEN-HEIRS WORLD SERIES
BOOK TWO

SARAH WESTILL

PERFECT MELODY SILENCED

Bella and the Beast Master – Book Two

Copyright 2023 by Sarah Westill

ISBN 978-1-955293-17-4

Cover Design by For the Muse Designs

OTHER TITLES BY SARAH WESTILL

GEN-HEIRS: The Guardians of Sziveria

(in reading order)

Levkaseon – A Prequel

Wintersfall

Raiventon

Kynhaven

Asherwick

Ericksen - A Wintervail Special

Survaine (April 27, 2023)

Bella and the Beast Master

A Gen-Heirs World series

Frozen Flowers Fallen

Perfect Melody Silenced

For world maps be sure to visit www.
sarahwestill.com

To get the latest updates, follow Sarah on
Instagram

@authorsarahwestill

OTHER TITLES BY SARAH WESTILL

GEN-HEIRS: The Guardians of Sziveria

(in reading order)

Levkaseon — A Prequel

Wintersfall

Raiventon

Kynhaven

Asherwick

Ericksen - A Wintervail Special

Survaine (April 27, 2023)

Bella and the Beast Master

A Gen-Heirs World series

Frozen Flowers Fallen

Perfect Melody Silenced

For world maps be sure to visit www.
sarahwestill.com

To get the latest updates, follow Sarah on
Instagram

@authorsarahwestill

Dedication and Acknowledgement

For Joseph, who thinks my created world is the most amazing thing ever and is always willing to help me imagine what a post-cataclysmic world would be like...

CONTENT WARNING:
This book contains mature content
Reader discretion is advised.

CHAPTER

ONE

P ort Scarbrough, Sziveria
September, 801P.C.E (Post-Cataclysmic Event)

AMONG THE FACES in the crowd awaiting the ship docking from Ruthenia, one was missing. Markus Ralston frowned, disappointment a sharp jab in his chest. Beside him, his Ruthenarc wolf Lunah jumped up and down, trying to see over the half wall.

Where is she, where? Lunah asked through their bond.

I don't know, Markus answered, leaning forward and resting his arms on the rail.

She knew we were arriving today, she knew?
Yes, she knew.

He'd sent Bella Fenwick a letter, and a radio message, letting her know a Sziverian family had contacted him to investigate the death of their daughter. Markus's assistance in April

1

with finding, and apprehending a serial killer, had led the desperate couple to seek him out and offer a reward for any information he could obtain concerning their daughter. Without a second thought, he jumped at having a legitimate excuse to return to the country.

To return to Bella.

The ship eased into position at the dock. Workers jumped into action attaching the plank for disembarking. A small group cheered on the wharf. They waved a pink banner and shouted. Seagulls dove and caught currents on their search for anything edible dropped by the people waiting. Their cries mingled with the ocean waves breaking on the wharf.

Markus and Lunah waited until the bulk of the passengers had gone ashore before venturing down the plank. The crowd had thinned to a few stranglers watching the ship for the passengers they awaited. Enough people had left to confirm Bella was indeed not present. Bag slung over his shoulder, Markus considered his next move. Ignore her lack of appearance and go meet the family hiring him, or seek her out.

On the way to the train station to go from the port to Haven City, his imagination went wild. Perhaps the scrawny *boy* behind the fence in evidence had finally managed to convince her to give him a yearlong marriage contract. Or the man she worked for, Guardian Reyes Avner, had wizened to what he'd had in front of him. Letters and radio messages couldn't compete with flesh and blood. By the time he hopped into the railcar, Markus had managed to convince himself Bella had a line of a marriage contracts waiting.

She is ours, she is, Lunah stated, her words calm and certain.

We've been gone months. A lot can happen in that time.

No. She punctuated the single word with a loud bark.

The passenger in front of them jumped and stared with big eyes over the top of the seat. Markus offered a toothy grin, which had the man spinning back around in his seat.

Markus scratched the top of her head. "We shall see."

No one took a seat beside him, not with Lunah at his feet, large and imposing. His silver and slate gray wolf stared anyone down who slowed, her golden eyes alert. As a Beast Master, he was awarded privileges where his animal was concerned. Their bond connected them on a physical level. When he concentrated hard enough, he could smell, hear and if she were far enough way, see all she did.

The train jerked into motion. Iron and steel squealed and grumbled. The release of brakes hissed. Markus swung his bag onto the empty seat next to him and focused on the Sziverian land sliding past his window. Untamed forest broken by rocky fields, with the occasional small city. Reminders of humanity's endurance nearly a millennia after an unknown event almost extinguished their race. Harsh arctic winters, and the arrival of a deadly sexually transmitted virus known as human rabies syndrome, served as continual reminders of life's fragile condition. Of the importance of living the gift given to each generation born in a world offered a second chance.

Markus didn't plan on squandering the potential future he'd found in Bella. Not that Lunah would allow him to. Despite all they both had to lose in a union outside of their own heritage. Over the long summer months separated from her, Markus had come to the conclusion only an outright rejection would stop him from pursuing the remarkable Sziverian. Even then, he'd figure a way to convince her to give them at least a year. The country had a funny way of doing relationships, but he'd take her any way he could get her.

Nature gave way to warehouses for the products being brought in from the ports to be distributed through the city and country. Warehouses transitioned into homes and businesses, coming closer and closer together until Haven City, the largest metropolis in the country, formed. The train slowed at the station, bustling with people. A sprawling glass canopy rose high above, keeping rain or snow off the patrons, but not warmth inside. Enclosed vendor booths provided an escape from the chill if necessary.

Adapted to the harsher climate of his

homeland, Markus remained unaffected by the dwindling temperatures of summer ushering in fall. The transitioning seasons meant a retreating window for him to return home. If he didn't find the answers the family wanted within three weeks, he'd be stuck in Sziveria until the spring thaw of the Northern Pass.

Rising when the train came to a complete stop, he hefted his pack onto his shoulder. Lunah stepped ahead of him and lead the way off the train. On the sidewalk in front of the station, Markus weighed the benefits of walking to the Sziverian National Investigative Division headquarters, or hiring a carriage. The slow-moving mixture of horse riders, bicyclists, passenger carriages, transportation carts, and the glimpse of an Ariot, a sleek magnetically powered, expensive and therefore rare, single passenger vehicle, made Markus turn right on the sidewalk. He pushed his way through others who opted to walk instead of ride.

Lunah's fur brushed his thigh with each step. He kept his fingers twined in the thick pelt between her shoulders. While she'd never wander, he liked to keep the reminder to remain close. A brisk wind blew leaves and common city debris around their feet. Lunah hopped over an empty, cracked glass jar. Her back feet sent it skittering and sliding between the people behind them. The delectable scent of bakery's competed with street vendors cooking meat or frying vegetables. Traffic crawled to a near stop closer to the government buildings. Tall and boring, cement block structures dominated several blocks, their rooftop greenhouses glittering like glass diamonds in the sky.

People entered and exited the SNID building. The warmth of the day failed to penetrate the deep shadows of the recessed doors. Markus waited for an opening in the constant flow of foot traffic to enter. Lunah took the opportunity for them, rushing the door at the first chance. Inside, Lunah sniffed the air, turning to the right when Markus would have gone straight to the stairs Bella preferred to use instead of the main stairway.

This way, her scent is this way, Lunah said.

Markus opened their bond, closing his eyes to better concentrate, and took in the sweet vanilla and berries of Bella lingering in the air among the hundreds of other scent trails. Like threads crossing over each other, all of them went gray while Bella's glowed a vibrant lavender. Sure enough, the thread led to the basement level, not the fifth floor, where she'd worked as a filing clerk for a lead investigative guardian on the serial crimes team. Markus hesitated.

Why would she be down there? he asked.

We won't know unless we go, we won't.

He sighed and pushed the door open to the wide, shadowed downstairs. Hanging lamps barely illuminated the inky depths. Following Lunah, they delved deeper into the underground labyrinth. Markus tried to remember what Bella had once told him was located on the lowest level. Evidence, which they headed away from. Supply, though he couldn't remember which direction she'd said to go if he ever had a need for paperclips. And long storage, where he wondered if she were located.

Light spilled from a door propped open by a wooden wedge shoved underneath. The whisper of shuffling paper broke the silence. Markus's bag bumped an over stacked shelving unit, causing boxes to rattle. He turned on his heel and held out his hands, making sure nothing fell.

"Intake is on the shelf to your left!" a female voice called. "If anything needs signed for, leave the slip and I'll have it delivered to your floor by the end of the day."

Lunah yipped and spun in an excited circle before taking off in the direction of the voice. A squeal of surprise turned into elated laughter, mingling with Lunah's overjoyed crying.

Happy! My Bella! Lunah chimed through their bond over and over again, making his heart twist.

The unfamiliar sensation of nerves left him motionless. For almost five months he'd been connected to her over letters. The anticipation of seeing her again had ruled his thoughts since learning he'd be returning to Sziveria. Now, with her feet away, he couldn't move. He didn't want to be treated like a stranger, yet what more could he expect? They'd spent a few days together solving a crime, in person they weren't any more familiar with each other than they'd been in the spring.

Lunah's happy exclamations faded and the rustle of papers sounded. Bella rounded a row of shelves, her dark curls haloed by a lamp behind her. She'd piled the unruly mass onto the top of her head. Most of the strands had escaped at the back and around her temples, leaving her beautiful face framed by whisps. Loose fitting cotton cream pants and a long-sleeved navy silk tunic flowed along her willowy frame. The clothes were more mature than her twenty-three years, and a bit too large for her. And still, she was the most beautiful woman he'd ever seen.

Markus didn't have time to speak. The moment her gaze met his, she broke into a run and launched herself at him. A quick reaction born from years of training allowed him to catch her instead of being thrown backward by the force of her momentum. Without thought, he picked her up. She wrapped around him, locking her ankles behind his back, her arms squeezing his shoulders. A faint tremble wracked her body as she buried her face in the crook of his neck.

Her embrace held a desperate edge. Markus hugged her tight to his chest. The warmth of her skin clung to the silk beneath his fingers. "What's wrong?" he whispered against her temple.

She shook her head and strengthened her

grip. Lunah sat at his feet, head tilted, a question in her golden eyes.

I don't know what is wrong, Markus said through their bond.

Bella leaned back enough for him to see her remarkable ocean green eyes, startling against her light brown skin. She touched his braid, his neck, the short hair of his beard. Then she shocked him to the center of his being by kissing him.

CHAPTER

TWO

Bella didn't think, she acted. Clinging to Markus like the lifeline he'd become, she allowed emotion to rule her and succumbed to the absolute need to kiss him. For five months she'd regretted not having allowed him more than the chaste peck he'd teased her with before he stepped onto a ship and sailed out of her life. The letters he'd written had only served to remind her what she already knew – she *missed* him.

His lips were firm beneath hers. The course bristles of his beard rubbed her chin and tickled her nose. The second she opened her mouth, her tongue touching to his bottom lip, he took over. Spinning them around, he pressed her to the wall beside the door. In the back of her mind, a sliver of alarm reminded her she was at work. A job she couldn't lose. An income she couldn't afford to be without. Then his tongue slid into her mouth, exploring and teasing in a seductive, dominating sensation she'd never experienced. The strength of his body came alive against hers. All rational thought fled as his kiss excited every nerve within her.

Bella could only hold on, his mouth slanting over hers, his kiss pulling her deeper and deeper into a vortex where only they existed. Markus tore his mouth from hers, his breathing heavy, his body still. Before Bella could react, he untangled her from around his frame and disappeared, melting into the shadows further into the room between shelving units, Lunah on his heels.

Blinking, Bella touched her shaky fingers to her damp lips. What just happened? She almost called out in her confusion when the faint echo of boots on the cement floor made her gasp. Dashing back to her work station, she wished she had a mirror to check her appearance. If the tingling of her lips and chin were any indication, she probably looked like she'd been well and thoroughly kissed. Which she had. She couldn't stop the small smile. Best kiss ever.

"Bella!" a familiar male voice shouted.

Keeping her sigh internal, Bella pulled a file box across her desk. "Over here, Guardian Avner."

Guardian Reyes Avner knew full well where her desk was located within the cavernous room. The same place all the other clerks before her had worked, and would work after her. Yet, they all did the same thing. Entered her little domain with a shout, reminding her of her place, and that to get any lower in position would mean being released. Avner came around the corner of tall file cabinets, a file in his hand. Bella kept her head down. The glossy sheen of his black shoes stopped inches from her.

"I need the evidence for these cases." He laid the folder on the desk. "C.G. said they'd all been placed in long storage."

"If they're over a decade, they'll be at the warehouse," she reminded him, picking up the file, still avoiding looking his direction.

"They aren't. I think the oldest one is four years. There hadn't been any movement on them in a year, so they were relocated here."

Bella went to the file system and pulled the location cards for the evidence he needed. "I'll be right back."

Avner sighed and sat in the only chair at her desk. Bella let loose her own sigh, but of relief and went in search of Markus. She found him peeking into a box, pulling a slip of lace out of the top. Exasperated, she popped the tips of her fingers on his wrist. When he looked at her in surprise, she shook her head and mouthed *no*. He slipped the lid back into place. She wanted to take the time to stare at him, to assure herself he really stood in front of her. All six-foot-five of un-tamed man. He'd cropped his beard, defining the angles of his jaw, which should have left him looking less wild. His fur-lined coat, long-braided hair, and eyes eerily close to the golden shade of his wolfs, detracted from any civility his trimmed facial hair may have provided.

Bella stepped close enough for her whisper to carry only between them. "Wait for me at my house, my shift ends at five."

"No, I'll wait here."

She glanced over her shoulder and listened. Anymore conversation was a risk she couldn't take. Nodding, she tapped the cards against her thigh and went in search of the required cases. Lunah shadowed her until she once again entered Avner's view. Confident she no longer appeared to have been doing something salacious in her workplace, Bella carried the boxes to her desk.

"Here's what I was able to find," she said, placing everything in front of him.

He stood, the light around them gleaming off his dark brown, well-groomed hair. Clean-shaven, wearing black slacks and a knitted cream sweater, Reyes Avner was the epitome of a Sziverian Guardian hopeful to achieve a ranked status in his career. Fit enough to not appear lazy, yet boasting evidence of a lifestyle lavish enough to afford excess weight, clothing of decent quality, he checked all the fashion boxes necessary to get him noticed. Either by his superiors, or a family already holding a ranking he could marry into. At one time, Bella had lamented being unable to be someone he could consider for a future. Good looks, good career, responsible, Avner had been the perfect idea of husband material.

Then Markus Ralston entered her life. And Avner became a poor example of masculine appeal. Not that her fantasies involving either of them would ever come to fruition. Bella knew her place in the world. At the bottom. She'd never be capable of holding a guardian position. Could never help a spouse achieve more.

Avner opened all the narrow boxes, poking around inside before closing them. "Perfect, thanks." He stacked them together and then tapped his fingers on the top lid. "The clerk they had replace you isn't half as good. I'm trying to get you reinstated." He offered a sideways smile. "Unless of course you prefer it down here."

Bella's brows lifted in surprise. "No, I don't. I appreciate it, thank you."

"I didn't agree with the change, but..." He shrugged.

She knew. Louder voices than his advocated for her demotion. He hadn't bothered to stand up for her, until now, when the inconvenience of her relegation to the basement had affected him. Bella smiled, not trusting herself to speak with the respect due his position. She grabbed a clipboard with the checkout sheet for evidence and held it out to him.

He set the clipboard on the top box and picked up one of the discarded pens from her desk. In his masculine, yet elegant script, he answered the questions, checked all the appropriate boxes, and then signed and dated the form. Bella did the same before adding the slip to the *Checked-Out* bin. Avner hesitated for a minute, his mouth opening, then he shook his head, gathered up the boxes and left. Bella let out a long exhale and collapsed in her chair.

Markus appeared between a row of shelves, Lunah at his side. Bella steeled her nerves and made herself busy. She collected the cards from requested evidence and stood.

"Sit back down," Markus ordered softly.

Ignoring him, she crossed the distance to the cataloging drawer cabinets. Her back to him, Bella returned the index cards to their proper drawers.

"Why are you down here? What did Guardian Avner mean when he said he didn't agree with the change?" Markus asked, his nearness bringing the alluring scent of a rain saturated forest.

"The lady who worked in here for thirty-one years retired four months ago. My organization skills made me a good fit, so here I am," she answered, filing the final card.

"Why are you lying?"

The harsh, yet lyrical notes of his accent made a shiver race up her spine. Bella loved the way he spoke, another thing she'd missed. She shrugged away his question and returned to her desk, continuing the sorting she'd been doing when Lunah had surprised her. "I'm not lying, Mrs. Carlson did retire and left a vacancy they needed filled."

He moved close to her again, his presence a warm heat at her back. "Why you? Anyone could label and store old evidence. You served a guardian, made sure he had what he needed to do his job to the best of his ability, and I *know* you did that well. Why would they take you from Avner?"

Bella swallowed away the tremble in her stomach. Bitterness and anger always filled her when she thought too hard about her new *position*. She didn't want to experience either in Markus's presence, she was too happy to see him again. Too thankful he'd returned. "I'm sorry I couldn't meet you at the port. I wanted to, but they wouldn't give me the time off."

"You were planning to?"

Relief filled her at his accepting the change in subject. "Of course I was."

He came around the desk and braced his hands on top of the papers she'd been organizing. Dipping his head, he met her gaze. His braid slid over his shoulder and brushed the documents. "Bella, why are you in the basement?"

A flush heated her face. Pressing her hands to her warm cheeks, she squeezed her eyes closed. "It doesn't matter."

Markus peeled one of her hands free and clasped her fingers until she looked at him again. "Tell me." When she didn't speak, he added, "Please."

"Markus," she whispered, "it doesn't matter. I have a job I'm thankful to be working.

Where in the building or in which position makes no difference."

He returned both hands to the desk, his jaw working as he pondered her. Bella knew how smart he was, how quick he could be to catch on to the smallest facts. Those perceptive eyes narrowed and her chest constricted. Alarm mingled with nervousness at the prospect of him guessing the reason for her demotion. She picked up an already labeled box needing shelved and turned away.

"They punished you for helping me," he said before she could escape. "Didn't they?"

Markus stared at Bella's back where she stood frozen between a row of shelving units. He stepped closer, Lunah slipping past to stand in front of Bella, blocking her in. "Am I right?"

"I said it doesn't matter," she murmured.

He grasped her upper arms from behind, his heart twisting. "Bella—"

"No," she interrupted, "there's nothing to discuss. You can't change anything. I didn't do anything wrong. But the guardians over the cases you helped solve in less than three days, when they'd been working on them for years, weren't happy. They didn't want to see me on their floor and they pushed hard to get me moved, which honestly, I was fine with. The hostility had become a bit more than I was willing to take."

His hands tightened on her arms. "They hurt you?"

A heavy sigh left her. "No. Just passive aggressive stuff, little things that made sure I knew I wasn't welcome on the fifth floor anymore."

She rolled her shoulders and he released his hold on a slow caress down her arms. The contents of the box jangled. Markus wrapped his arms around her and took hold before she could object, lifting the container over her head. "Where do you need this?"

"I can handle carrying a box."

"I know," he said. "But I'm ready to leave, so let's get your work done."

"I have to stay until my shift is over."

Markus glanced around, found an opening on a shelf, and shoved the box into the space. "I need your help on this case I've taken."

She let out a low grumble, pulling the box from the spot. "And I need this job. I'll be off in two hours. You can wait in here, or wherever you want."

He looked around the dim, narrow aisles, the shelves packed to the point of excessive, and fought off the sense of claustrophobia. "How long have you been stuck down here?"

Moving along the row, she searched the labels. She stopped near the end and braced the box between her hip and a shelf, lifting her thigh to prop it in place. With a remarkable display of balance, she maneuvered objects around to make space. "I told you, four months."

Markus thought back over their conversation. "No, you said the lady retired four months ago."

"Yes, and they moved me into her position." She nudged the evidence into the hole she'd made and then stood back and observed her work. Shaking her head, she adjusted the box and the other objects sharing the space. Afterward, seeming to be satisfied, she wrote on a small card attached to the shelf.

Markus trailed after her down the aisle, while Lunah sniffed ahead, never more than a few feet from them. The enticing memory of her kiss made him want a repeat. He had a daring urge to tempt her. "If you won't leave with me, then can we spend the next two hours kissing?"

"Markus!" She laughed. "What are you, sixteen?"

He stopped close to her back and resisted the need to touch her. "Sixteen is not an exclusive age for wanting to kiss someone."

She glanced over her shoulder at him, her brows drawn. "No, but it is an age where you can neglect responsibility in favor of doing nothing more than making out."

"I want to kiss you," he whispered into her ear.

"No." She laughed again. "I do have to work." To punctuate the statement, she stopped to organize a section of shelves. He noted the faint tremble of her hands with a smirk of satisfaction. She wasn't as unaffected as she wanted him to believe.

Lunah let loose a loud whining yawn, her sharp teeth gleaming in the lamplight. Bella continued to pretend he didn't stand inches behind her. Keeping his frustration internal, Markus headed back to her desk.

Come on, Lunah, he said, *leave Bella to her work.*

Boring work, boring, the wolf quipped, her words followed by a faint yip.

Markus agreed. At Bella's desk, he dropped into the chair, sending the wooden legs screeching across the cement floor. Lunah shook her head, her ears smacking. Markus tapped his knuckles on the file and paper covered desk. He opened random drawers and dug around inside until he found a roll of paper tape. Twisting the roll between his fingers, he contemplated Lunah.

Want to play? he asked, brow raised.

She lowered her torso to the floor, tail wagging, and barked two high pitched yelps. Smiling, Markus unwound the tape, forming a ball in his palm. He tested the creation a few times, adding layers as needed until satisfied. New toy in hand, he rose, wiggled it in front of Lunah's nose and then sent it flying down a long aisle to his right. Lunah bolted after the ball, her nails scrambling to catch purchase on the smooth textured floor. Mindful of the rows and how one well-placed body slam from his large

Ruthenarc wolf could send the shelves tumbling like dominoes, he kept his throws straight.

Lunah found unique ways to return, even attempting to sneak up behind him on one run. Markus used their bond to learn where she'd appear from. At the last moment, he turned, arms out, and caught her as she launched herself at him, the ball of tape in her mouth. Laughing, Markus wrapped his arms around her furry body. The impact of her weight sent him stumbling backward, into the desk.

Cheater, you are a cheater, Lunah scolded through their link. The ball fell from her mouth and rolled down his chest while she nipped at his jaw.

Markus hugged her tighter, burying his face in the thick fur at her neck. "Not a cheater," he said. "Remember what I always tell you, use everything you have to be victorious."

She twisted her head and grabbed his jacket sleeve. Growling, she tugged on the fabric. Markus growled back and grasped her muzzle, giving a gentle squeeze and playful shake.

"You treat her like she's young," Bella said, a box perched on her hip.

Markus gave Lunah's muzzle another teasing shake before pushing her away. "She's almost five, young by Ruthenarc wolf standards. She's not a normal dog breed, and is still learning from me. We haven't been in many field situations."

Bella set the box on the desk and rested her forearm on top. "I remember you saying her lifespan could be the same as yours."

"*Dak*." He scratched between Lunah's ears. Her tongue lolled from her mouth. "Life happens, however. Our work is not always safe. She's my third wolf to bond with."

"What happened to your other two wolves?" she asked, shifting her position to lean over, crossing her arms to brace them both on the box.

Anxiety spiked through him at her question. Lunah licked his forearm. "I lost both of them in separate conflicts with New Columbia."

She frowned. "That had to have been hard."

Markus grabbed Lunah's face in both his hands, his gaze meeting her luminous golden eyes. "It was traumatic. I was nineteen when I lost my first wolf. My commander had to knock me out when my bond with Atlas snapped. I went a little crazy. I did better when Thebe died, only passing out for a few minutes."

"How old were you then?" she asked gently, her eyes soft with compassion.

"Twenty-six." He stroked up Lunah's velvety, fuzzy ears, comforted by the weight of their bond. "I waited as long as I could before going to a breeder to find a new pup. If I didn't need to be bonded to function, I wouldn't have taken on another wolf. I opted to resign from my position as a Ground Commander when I found Lunah, and I help in pretty much the same capacity as your Arch Guardian Wolven-guard, now."

"Convict recovery and criminal investigation assistance?" she asked, smiling.

"Yeah, all of that. Missing persons, too."

Bella straightened, pulling the box to the edge of the desk and popping the lid off. "She's a puppy still, then?"

"A juvenile. She won't reach full maturity for another ten years."

Her hand froze halfway to the box as she looked at him. "Ten years?"

"*Dak*." Markus bumped Lunah to step back, and picked up the ball of tape. "My other two wolves never made it into their equivalent of adulthood. I have other plans for Lunah."

Bella's gaze wandered over the wolf. "Will she change any?"

"Not on the outside, no. But like a human, her capacity to reason and understand will increase, and of course, she'll be able to breed."

"Will you?"

He raised his brows in a silent question.

Bella titled her hand toward Lunah. "Breed her."

"Ah." He grasped Lunah's muzzle and shook her head side-to-side, earning a playful growl. "That's complicated. Most beast masters don't, unless they bond with another master who has a wolf of the opposite gender, then maybe. We can't exactly *home* any pup-pies, as they must go to other beast masters capable of wolf bonds. If a wolf proves to have remarkable traits, it may be requested to breed, though."

Bella reached into the box and pulled out several files and wrapped packages. "I bet they'll ask you about Lunah. She's remarkable."

"That may be true," he conceded, partial as he was to his wolf. "But I don't know if I'd be able to part with any of her offspring. And I can't keep a wolf pack."

She opened a file and flipped through the pages. Without looking up, she asked, "Why not?"

"Could you give up any of your children?"

Her gaze snapped to him. "They'd be puppies."

Markus leaned forward until his nose nearly touched hers. "They'd be *her* puppies. I am linked to her. Every moment of delight she experienced with her litter, every frustration, I'd share. They'd be mine as much as hers. By the time she was ready to part with the pups, I'd be too attached to let any of them go. The same will be true for any children I have, they will be Lunah's, too."

She used her fingers to mark her place in the folder and perched on the edge of the desk, the file resting on top of her thigh. "You never explained your bond with her. Not even in your letters. Will you tell me now?"

Close enough to discern the subtle nui-sances in her ocean green eyes, Markus almost forgot what she asked. He blinked and straightened, putting space between them. If he stayed too close, he'd taste her lips again. Chances were, with no one around and a flat surface at his disposal, he wouldn't stop at kissing. "No, you're working."

Bella's fingers tightened on the folder to keep from smacking Markus. Or throwing it at him. The urge to do either had her teeth grinding. "Right, I am."

"You needed the reminder as much as I did," he said quietly. "I really want to kiss you."

Her heart kicked a hard *thump* into her ribs. She shifted off the desk, opening the file to give her something, anything, to focus on besides the memory of his tongue doing deli-cious things inside her mouth. "I have to sort this box, it was miscategorized, then I can leave."

Both his hands disappeared inside and she laughed.

"I can handle it," she said.

"And if I help, we can leave sooner. I really want you at this meeting I have with the family who hired me."

Bella closed the file, wrote the proper infor-mation on the tab, and set it in the bin to be stored. "They hired you, not me."

He grasped her chin and forced her to meet

his intense golden stare. "Are you on the verge of telling me you won't be of any use?"

If you say you're a nobody again, I will kiss you.

His promise from months ago reflected in his eyes. Bella shook her head.

In a gentle caress, his hold released her chin. "Good."

"Why is my going so important to you?" she asked.

"I told you six months ago, Bella. You *see*. I need your perception. I need to know what everyone else has missed."

Bella rubbed at her temples. Six months ago, she'd seen something no one else had and Markus was the only one who took her seriously. Who'd listened and used what she'd found to catch a killer. She worried he misconstrued her brief flash of insight for something she wasn't.

Bella filed. She was a clerk. At one time, she'd been a personal assistant to Guardian Reyes Avner, a team leader for a serial crime's unit at the SNID. Aside from being the personal assistant to a ranked guardian, she'd never hold a higher position.

When her parents had her tested for genetically inherited traits at sixteen, she'd scored high enough to qualify for an administrative role, but not for a guardian position. Unlike Markus, she wasn't a Gen-Heir. Her quirky talent of being able to visualize herself within a painting or drawing, as though she really stood inside the confines of the artist's vision, didn't count for anything.

Markus disagreed.

He claimed to see something in her gift, in *her*. When he finally realized how ordinary she was, she feared his disappointment. The more he insisted on her assistance, the closer the moment would arrive. Bella wanted to say no. To remain in her safe, little clerical job, which she needed.

But his presence caused an unfamiliar need, and the thought of being separate from him a strange anxiety. An odd compulsion practically demanded she stay with him. Not to mention, she couldn't deny his conviction in her felt good. She wanted to be who he saw, even if it wasn't the truth. His perception was a lie she couldn't afford to accept, and a danger she couldn't allow.

"Get out of your head," he said, laying a file on top of the one she'd set to be re-catalogued. "Your argument with yourself won't be won."

"I wasn't..." He cast her a skeptical look, complete with a raised brow. She flushed and cleared her throat. "Fine, I was, but it's your fault."

"The first of many offenses I'm sure to unknowingly commit." He *tsked*. "Should I apologize?"

"Somehow I don't think I could get you to," she mumbled.

"You're right," he proclaimed, dropping another stack of papers with a flourish. "Since I'm sure you're wanting me to think you aren't smart, insightful, or talented, I wouldn't apologize for feeling that way. You are all those things, and probably many more, which I can't wait to discover."

Bella stared at him. "No wonder you have such a good wolf, do you praise her like this?"

"When she deserves it, yes. Everyone should know their strengths, and their weaknesses. How do you learn them if you aren't told?"

How indeed. Bella knew her strengths, and weaknesses. One such weakness stood within touching distance.

"Your mother knows you're special," he continued before she could speak. "And I know despite her efforts to get you to believe it, too, you won't. I'm going to figure out how to prove to you that you *are* gifted, and you should be one of the guardians your country holds in such high esteem."

Propping her hand on her hip, she faced him. "And if I'm not? If there's nothing to discover and I'm just common Bella Fenwick?"

His knuckles brushed down her cheek and caressed her jaw, his eyes searching her face. "Never common."

Bella couldn't help leaning into his touch. Once again, her chest tightened at how much she'd missed him. She wanted to give in to both their urges and climb his body and claim his mouth a second time. Knowing he'd let her, made her take a careful step away.

Lunah licked her fingers, drawing Bella's attention.

"She thinks Bella Fenwick is amazing," Markus whispered. "We both do."

"Amazing is the ability to communicate with a wolf," Bella clarified, gathering the folders ready to be stored. Keeping her back to them, afraid they'd witness the tears burning in her eyes, she went to the long wall of filing cabinets. Their joint affection for her did sappy things to her heart.

The faint *click* of Lunah's nails on the cement floor followed her. She didn't dare check to see if Markus also trailed behind. The man had an uncanny ability to walk in silence. After filing, she turned and found Lunah watching her, but no Markus. The huge wolfdog reached nearly to Bella's chest when she sat, making petting her easy. Smoothing her fingers between Lunah's ears, Bella smiled.

"I bet you're ready to get out of this dark basement, huh?"

Lunah woofed softly.

"I'll take that as a yes. All right, let's go find your Markus."

When they didn't find him at her desk, Lunah lifted her head, cocked her ears, and headed down a row. They found him placing the box she'd been emptying on a shelf in the Financial Crimes section of storage. Each unit had its own space. She raised her brows at him knowing where the box had belonged. Someone had dumped random files and evidence into it and placed the container in Intelligence. After ensuring nothing had been intentionally hidden, she'd sorted everything with Markus.

"How did you know where that went?" she asked.

"I know money numbers when I see them."

Bella patted and then rubbed Lunah's head. The dog graced her with a happy smile. "Your wolf is ready to go."

He lifted his brows. "We can leave?"

"Yes."

He disappeared and returned with a bulky bag slung over his shoulder. With a sweep of his hand, he motioned for her to precede him. Bella ran to her desk and grabbed her bag and jacket. The autumn days cooled to uncomfortable temperatures once the sun set. Lunah trotted ahead, leading the way without error.

The usual crowd in the lobby had thinned to those leaving later than normal for the season. Ice would form soon after sunset. While cold enough for frost, this time of year the roads were still accessible. In a few weeks the conditions would worsen, and no one would dare leave late.

Someone's heels clicked a heavy staccato across the polished tile floor. Bella glanced towards the wide stairs leading to the floors above. Guardian Marion Hinke dug around inside her purse. The urge to hide had Bella searching frantically for an alcove, open room, even the space underneath a desk would work.

Displaying the same eerie skill he'd had earlier, Markus grabbed the back of her jacket and pulled her close.

"Does she scare you?" he whispered. The warmth of his breath across her ear sent a shiver along her spine.

"She hates me," Bella said. "If it had been up to her, I wouldn't have even been relegated to the basement, I'd have been fired."

"For helping me stop an international incident?" He shook his head. "That's ridiculous. She must have been jealous."

"I don't care what she was, I don't want her to see me," Bella stressed under her breath.

"You have as much right to be here as she does," Markus declared, his hand sliding from between her shoulder blades to the small of her back.

Lunah's tail brushed Bella's thigh before she sat, blocking Bella's escape unless she wanted to return to the basement. The huge wolf tilted her head, a pleased look shining in her gaze. Bella glared, not phasing Lunah one bit. Maybe she'd be fortunate and the rude, spiteful guardian would keep walking, too wrapped up in her own sense of self to notice them.

No such luck. Guardian Hinke lifted her head. Her focus zeroed in on Bella before sliding to Markus and down to Lunah. Disdain twisted her sharp features into a sneer. Hand still in her purse, she stopped a few feet from them. "I see the savage has returned for his little snoop. Couldn't get enough information via letters? Had to return and see what other accolades she could help you achieve?" Hinke's contempt intensified as her gaze settled on Bella. "And you, still working against the guardians to further yourself. How pathetic."

Bella reeled at the spite-filled words and downright loathing emanating from the guardian. Marion Hinke had seemed to dislike Bella from her first day serving Guardian Avner, predicting Bella would only last a week in the demanding serial crimes unit. Meanwhile, neither Marion nor Reyes had been promoted to a ranked position, which in Bella's opinion only made the woman nastier.

"Why I'm here is of no concern to you and doesn't involve your division this time," Markus stated calmly.

"Then why show up here at all?" Marion asked, crossing her arms over her chest.

"Again, not your business."

Marion's dark brown eyes narrowed. "So, you're not here for an investigation?"

"We were on our way out," Bella said. She wrapped her arm around Markus and tugged him toward the front door.

"You're taking an awful risk associating with him," Marion pressed. "I *know* you can't afford to lose your job, Miss Fenwick."

"Associating with Markus won't cost me my job, Guardian Hinke."

"Unless he asks you to find information for him that hasn't been authorized."

Bella bit back a scoff. "He wouldn't do that because he knows I won't agree."

"I'm right here," Markus said in disbelief. "If you have a problem with me, Guardian Hinke, say it to my face."

"I think you're a barbarian who could care less about our rules and civility and will do whatever you want to make sure you succeed," Marion snapped. Her eyes widened and she returned her attention to Bella. "Is he paying you? Is that why you're helping him? How much of the reward did he send you last time?"

Bella blinked. "Reward? There wasn't a reward."

"There was in Ruthenia," Marion quipped, lifting her chin. "You think he solved that crime from the goodness of his nature?"

"Yes," Bella said without pause.

"Then you're more naïve than I thought. You're going to regret working with him," Marion said, her chin lifting higher, before she stalked off.

Bella blew out a frustrated breath. "I'm sorry."

"What are you apologizing for? Her being an awful human? That is not your fault." Markus took her hand from his arm and squeezed. "Does she always cause trouble for you like this?"

"If I see her, yes. I think she forgets about me until then. Thankfully, she's only needed something once from long storage. When I didn't find it fast enough, she wrote a complaint."

"Bella…"

Shaking her head, Bella once again tried to leave. "No, there's nothing anyone can do. She's decided I'm her enemy and nothing I do will change her mind."

He remained rooted in place, still holding her hand, forcing her to stop. "You shouldn't have to work around such hostility."

"She's one person in a building of hundreds. Everyone else treats me just fine."

Skepticism pinched his features and filled his eyes as he looked at her for a long moment. Then he shook his head and lifted his hand. "Let's go then."

Bella didn't need to be told twice.

CHAPTER

THREE

Markus helped Bella from the hired carriage onto a narrow sidewalk. Primroses in oranges, pinks and startling blues framed the walkway from the road to a large two-story gray stone house. Pillars supported a second-story greenhouse balcony stretching the width of the house. Frost impervious plants filled the porch in pots, mounted boxes and hanging baskets. Every plant thrived.

"I think we're about to meet a Gen-Heir botanist," Markus said, paying the driver.

"I hope it's not Hayden Jossern," Bella said.

"It's not. The family name is Vanscoyn."

"I haven't heard of them."

"Really?" Markus said, surprised. "Their daughter, Linettie Vanscoyn was a rising star in the music field."

Bella observed the house, shielding her eyes from the late afternoon sun glaring between houses. "I don't follow music much. Now art..."

"I remember."

She smiled. "Yes, I know."

The door opened when they were halfway up the walk. A fit, middle-aged man met them at the top of the porch steps, his hand held out in welcome. Lunah squeezed between them, hanging back as Markus took the lead and accepted their hosts greeting.

"Markus Ralston, and my wolf, Lunah," he said, and then motioned to Bella. "This is Bella Fenwick."

"Banks Vanscoyn," he returned in introduction. "Very happy you agreed to take on our case, Mr. Ralston. My wife, Tamie, is inside. All of this is her doing." He gestured around the porch. "Since we lost Netti, she hasn't stopped growing things."

"Is she a botanist?" Bella asked.

Banks shook his head, shoving a hand in his front pocket while opened the door for them. "No. She was a costume designer for the performance market. She'd designed all the gowns Netti wore while performing, along with several other well-known singers and actresses. After our daughter died, she retired and started planting."

Markus stepped to the side for Lunah to enter first, followed by Bella. Her shocked gasp mirrored his own astonishment at the volume of flora overtaking the interior of the house. Crowding all the available space before windows, between furniture, and even suspended from the ceiling in baskets or rope-hanging pots, trees, flowers, vines, and leafy plants occupied the home. Everywhere he looked, something green filled his vision.

Wet soil clumped to her wrists and sticking to her fingers, a woman stooped over a large pot braced on an iron pedestal. A long braid of fading dark brown hair dangled to her hips. An apron streaked with dirt covered her gray slacks and the orange sweater she had pushed to her elbows. She hummed an unfamiliar tune.

"Tamie darling," Banks said, easing past them into the spacious living room, "the investigator and his assistant have arrived."

The woman didn't stop her humming, or her attention to her plant. Banks waited for a minute before sighing and shaking his head. Dejection darkened his face and he waved for them to follow him. They ventured without his wife into the next room, a den with only a few plants and limited natural light.

"I'm sorry," he said, taking a seat in one of four large padded chairs. "I'd hoped once you arrived and she knew I was serious about learning the truth concerning our daughter's death, she'd respond in some manner."

"She's always that preoccupied?" Markus asked, sitting across from Banks and setting his bag on the floor to his left. Lunah waited until Bella sat on his right before laying in the small space between their chairs.

Banks ran both his hands down his face. "Yes. She woke up five months ago, said she was going to buy some plants, and hasn't done anything else since. I lost my wife when I lost my daughter."

Sympathy filled Markus. "Learning the truth about your daughter may not change anything for your wife."

"I know," he said on a sad exhale. "But I can try. I have to try."

Markus pulled a notebook from his inner jacket pocket and flipped to the first clean page. He jotted down the date and the name of the client. "Then let's get started. Tell me about your daughter."

Banks rose and went behind a small desk at the back of the room. "I have a box of her things here for you. I gathered all the articles written about her, her lyric journals, some of her favorite books, programs from all the shows she'd been to, along with anything else you'd mentioned may be helpful."

"She died in Sziveria?" Markus asked.

"Yes," he said, setting the box on the floor at Markus's feet. Bella grasped the lid and pulled it closer to her. "After a show in Monaco Sands." Banks looked at Bella, pride shining in his eyes. "Getting an invite to perform at one of the venues in Monaco Sands was a career maker for any singer. Netti was over the moon, and her performance, as you'll see in the articles, was praised to be one of the best in her generation. The critics claimed she had a true genetic gift that would only grow as her voice continued to mature. A promising new talent, and rising star to watch for years to come. She'd only been home for a day."

Bella placed the box on her lap. "Was there an investigation?"

"Haven City Enforcement Services did come out, but they declared her death accidental," Banks answered.

"Do you have their official report?" Markus asked.

"I don't, no." He stood and went back to his desk. "I can give you the name of the enforceman who came to the house." A drawer squeaked open, followed by rustling as he rummaged around. "Ah, here we are." He stood, a scrap of paper between his fingers. "An investigator is sent for all deaths, and Key Guardian Prine handled Netti's case."

Markus accepted the information, reading over the quick, masculine scrawl. "Key Guardian Prine, Waldon Nossman, who also holds the position as Tribunii within the HCES. Lots of names to remember."

"Yes," Bella agreed. "An enforceman can hold both a ranked guardian position, and of course, has a position within Enforcement Services. Many are only guardians, however. They don't hold a guardian ranking."

"I prefer the much simpler position acknowledgement in Ruthenia," Markus said, shaking his head.

"I know we're convoluted," Bella said. "But

it's a way to remember our heritage. To know who the first families were to step up and become guardians of our country."

Markus returned his attention to Banks. "You said over our radio transmissions, your daughter was found in her bathtub? So it was here, in this house?"

"Yes. Tamie found her when she didn't come down to dinner. Key Guardian Prine suspected she'd been dead for almost two hours by that point."

Markus wrote the information in his notebook. "What about a scene sketch?"

"They did one single sketch, I think," Banks said, his gaze unfocused in thought. "Yes, just one, in case the autopsy results were unexpected."

"And the results weren't unusual according to them," Markus stated.

"Correct." Banks rubbed his thumb and middle finger across his forehead, fatigue deepening the faint lines on his face. "I know my daughter didn't drown in that tub by accident. But I don't know how to prove it. I searched that bathroom myself and found nothing."

"If there's anything to find, I will," Markus assured. "If it was an accident after all, we'll discover that, too."

Banks dropped his hand to his lap and looked through the open door of the den into the living space. "Accident or something more sinister, I don't know now if either answer will help my Tamie. Losing Linettie broke something inside her."

"I can't imagine losing a child," Bella whispered. "The horror and heartache... I'm so sorry. I know that's not enough."

"Help us find answers," Banks said, returning his attention to them. He opened his hands in supplication. "Just help us know what happened."

CHAOS REIGNED at the Central Lane Division of Haven City Enforcement Services. The corridor Bella attempted to navigate ahead of him was packed with people vying to be heard at nearly every door. The rule requiring proof of guilt meant before an accusation could even be leveled, evidence had to be submitted, and could be argued against. Every petty thief, domestic dispute, forger, minor crimes, and from the sounds of some shouting, not so minor, clamored to be heard among those hoping for the case to continue on to an accusation hearing.

Too many sounds, too many smells, too many, Lunah whined.

I can take you outside, or up to the greenhouse, Markus offered.

Bella must come with us, Bella must. I do not want her here alone, I do not.

Markus agreed. The need to be in her presence had grown stronger after their kiss. He didn't know what he was going to do come tonight when he had to part ways with her.

And damn it, the sensual memory of her kiss had him wanting to taste her again. Longer. Deeper.

Forcing his attention back to the loud, obnoxious crowd, Markus sent an order to his wolf. *Lunah, straes'ya zre archen'ya caz Bella.*

A sharp yip acknowledged his command to seek and return with Bella. Finding an open space against the nearest wall, he waited for them. The crowd parted with grumbles of complaint. Lunah held the bottom of Bella's tunic sweater in her muzzle, doubling the space required for them to pass. Exasperation shone in Bella's eyes and tightened her mouth.

"You can tell her to let go now," Bella said, frowning.

Markus raised a brow and glanced at Lunah. "She wants to make sure you follow us to the greenhouse. The noise and scents are too much for her in here."

Swiping her hand between her shirt and Lunah's mouth, she made the wolf release her hold. Bella leaned over and grasped Lunah's ears in a gentle hold and brought her muzzle close. "Of course, I will walk with you." She placed a kiss between Lunah's eyes.

My Bella, mine, Lunah said.

Markus ruffled the dense fur at the base of her neck. *She is neither of ours.*

Lunah growled softly. A woman close to them took an alarmed step away. Markus tightened his fingers.

Behave, he ordered.

Lunah snapped her jaw, but made no other noises. Bella looked between them.

"Is everything okay?" she asked.

"Fine," Markus said, offering a faint smile. "Shall we?"

"The greenhouse is on the top floor, just like the SNID building."

"All your government buildings have them on the roof?"

"Yes. When the days turn too cold to venture outside, the greenhouses provide a much-needed break."

Bella led them to the nearest set of emergency stairs, less busy than the main flight of steps. Up at the top, Bella held the door for Lunah. Warm, moist, dirt scented air swirled around the opening. Markus followed a path made of bark around, ensuring Lunah would be alone. Short trees, potted flowers, and benches set in greenery, or overlooking the city, created an escape. Back at the door, he knelt in front Lunah and rubbed her ears.

Be good, I'll let you know when we return.

She chuffed in acknowledgement. Bella lingered in the doorway, her attention on Lunah's retreating form.

"She'll be okay in here by herself?" Bella asked.

"*Dak*, better than in the crowd downstairs."

Bella chewed on her bottom lip. "I can stay with her, if you want to go speak with the key guardian."

Warmth spread through his chest at her concern for his wolf. He regarded her thoughtfully. "You don't want to hear what he says?"

Her focus remained in the greenhouse. "It's not my investigation..."

"And you don't want to leave her," Markus finished for her quietly.

Bella wrapped her arms around her waist, her forehead pinched in confusion. "I don't, and I'm not sure why."

Markus couldn't stop himself from cupping her jaw and pulling her face close. He looked deep into her aquamarine eyes and pressed a soft kiss to her lips. "I do."

"Why?" she whispered against his mouth, her gaze questioning.

Markus shook his head. "I'll explain later."

"There's something to explain?" she asked, her eyes widening.

"Maybe, maybe not. Now isn't the time, though."

No, now definitely wasn't the time to tell Bella his wolf was in the process of developing an unbreakable bond with her. A situation Markus had never dreamed possible outside his motherland. One he still hadn't decided what to do about. He couldn't deny his growing attraction, or the insatiable desire to be around the pretty Sziverian. The predicament wasn't one he could concern himself with, though. Not yet. But soon he knew he'd have no choice.

Bella pulled away, her hands gripping the

strap of her bag. "I'm going to stay, and we can talk about why I can't seem to make a different choice tonight."

"All right," Markus agreed. "I'm looking forward to seeing your mother."

Bella laughed, and reaching out she brushed the trimmed beard covering his jaw. "So polite. Where is this savage Guardian Hinke seems convinced lurks inside you, hmm?"

Markus grasped her hand and nipped at the tip of her fingers. He let the lust he couldn't deny for the woman standing before him rise in his gaze. Her breath left her on a ragged exhale. Markus wanted to inhale her. To pick her up, feel her pressed against his chest again, and taste her sweetness. "It's here, I promise."

"You better go," she said, breathless. "The guardian won't be around much longer."

His focus shifted to the sky beyond the greenhouse windows. Orange and pink lightened the clouds against a darkening blue horizon. "All right, but don't leave the greenhouse."

A playful gleam brightened her eyes. She pressed a hand to her chest and bowed. "Yes, beast master."

Markus rolled his eyes and dragged her into a hug. Laughing, she wrapped her arms around his waist and squeezed. The simple, teasing moment felt comfortable. Right. Markus imagined life with Bella would never be boring, or without laughter. And why, until now, had he thought he'd ever want anything less?

When he thought of his future mate prior to meeting Bella, he figured the relationship would be built on respect and the bond neither of them would be able to deny. Love, laughter, perhaps even passion, weren't things that always came into consideration when mates were found between beast masters. The mating happened, their wolves accepted, the bond formed, and if they were fortunate, a family would arise.

The link between them ensured neither could stray, keeping them safe from the dreaded, and deadly, human rabies syndrome. Each civilization dealt differently with the sexually transmitted virus. Ruthenia had little need to cope, since most couples developed an inseparable connection which lasted for life.

He gave Bella one more quick hug before releasing her and heading back to the third floor where the key guardian worked. He'd worry about relationships and complicated bonds later. Despite the hour nearing for sunset, and therefore cold traveling conditions, the crowd in the corridor hadn't thinned. Markus pushed his way through until he found the placard with the key guardian's name above an office door. He rapped his knuckles on the frame and waited for the man hunched over the desk to notice him. Two hanging lanterns over the desk illuminated the windowless room and made the guardian's blond hair appear ashy.

Key Guardian Prine, Walden Nossman, looked up and frowned. Rising, he took Markus in, laying both his hands flat on the desk. Wrinkles covered a pale blue shirt too big for his frame, and slate gray slacks hung from his lean hips, barely staying up with the help of a brown leather belt. "Do you have an appointment?"

"No," Markus said. "I'm here to ask about a death you cleared as accidental. I've been hired by the family."

Somehow the man managed to pull off both surprise and disgust, his head snapping back and his dark eyes narrowing. "A reward seeker."

"I sought nothing," Markus clarified. "They reached out to me, I accepted."

The key guardian looked him over once more, his bulbous nose wrinkling. "You're not from here."

Markus wanted to ask if his genetic inheritance led him to that conclusion, but instead said, "I'm from Ruthenia. My wolf is upstairs, in the greenhouse."

Nossman swallowed, his Adams apple jutting from his pale, slender neck. "Ah, you're a beast master."

Tilting his head in acknowledgment, Markus pulled out his notebook. "Can you speak with me?"

"If the death was accidental, all the case

information will be filed with the records department."

Markus paused opening his notes. "Even the scene sketch?"

"Oh, no, we don't usually include those due to their graphic nature. I can see if I have a copy." Nossman rounded his desk and went to the center file cabinet out of three. Metal squealed as he opened a drawer. "What is the name?"

"Vanscoyn."

Nossman muttered to himself while searching through the files. Sweat stained the pits of his shirt and dotted the back. Closer to the guardian, Markus noted he had at least six inches on him, and probably a hundred pounds. Lunah might outweigh the slim man. Paper whispered as Nossman pulled a file free. He flipped through the first couple pages and removed a few.

"Here you are, the scene sketches."

Markus raised his brows, accepting the papers. "I was told only one was made."

Nossman tapped the pages. "No, the artist drew the scene from two angles, and how the body was found."

"Fantastic, thank you." Markus tucked the pages under his arm and opened his notebook. "Is your full report available at the records department?"

Crossing his arms, Nossmam leaned against the cabinet. "There wasn't much to report. The woman was found in her bathtub by her mother. No signs of a struggle. Nothing suspicious about the parents, or the household staff."

Markus made quick notes. "She hadn't had any issues with admirers?"

The guardian shook his head. "No, none. If I remember correctly, her career hadn't reached the same heights here in Sziveria that she'd achieved in Monaco Sands, or even southern Westica, where her parents had said she'd toured before her contract for a month of shows in Monaco Sands."

"Where she'd received high accolades."

"That's what they said, yes."

"What was your personal assessment of the scene?" Markus asked.

"She'd only been home a single day. She was stressed, took some valerian, scented her water with lavender, and fell into deep sleep, drowning," he answered without hesitation. "The medical science investigator agreed, ruling her death accidental. There's nothing much else to add."

Markus noted the guardian's words. "Thank you." He read the remarks so far, and then swapped the notebook for the scene sketches. Looking over each one carefully, he asked, "Where was the valerian she took found?"

"In her bedroom, on the nightstand." Nossman turned around and opened the drawer again. He dug around inside. "I'm sure I made a note of that in my report."

Markus waited while the Guardian searched the file.

A heavy frown darkened Nossman's face. "I'm positive I saw the medication next to her bed."

"The scene artist only drew the bathroom," Markus said. "And I don't see any medicine."

Nossman shrugged and returned the file to the drawer. "Oh well, I didn't make a note, but I did see the valerian, that's how I knew she'd taken some."

Five months ago, Markus had noted a general apathy when it came to investigating in Sziveria. Either the investigators found something, or they didn't, there wasn't much proactive response to solving a crime. In the case where a crime didn't appear to happen at all, they apparently didn't bother to ensure the situation was indeed what it seemed. Markus understood the Vanscoyn's desire to learn more information about their daughter's death. The answers they'd received from the investigation were limited.

"Will you be available if I have any additional questions?" Markus asked, returning his notebook to his jacket.

Nossman rubbed the back of his neck. "Sure, If I'm here."

Agitated by the guardian's lack of concern, Markus muttered his thanks again instead of barking out his frustration. In the corridor, he navigated the crush of people to the emergency stairs. The quiet solitude was a much welcome reprieve. Taking the stairs to the top floor two at a time, he let his anticipation at seeing Bella and Lunah replace his displeasure.

The humid, earth-scented air surrounded him as he stepped inside the greenhouse. Markus spotted Bella immediately, standing in the center of a path not far from him. Facing away, her hands were braced on her slender hips. Lunah was nowhere in sight.

"Where are you? You sneaky wolf," Bella muttered.

"What's going on?" he asked, looking around for his wolf.

"We're playing hide-and-seek. I found her the first three times, but somehow she's managed to disappear for this round," Bella answered. "No one else has come in, so I know she didn't sneak out."

"She wouldn't have anyway," Markus assured. "She said she'd stay here, and she wouldn't leave you."

"Even if she thinks it's all still a game?" Bella sighed and turned in a circle.

Markus worked his jaw in thought. "She's not far, she'd still want to see you."

Crouching, she angled her head. "I already checked underneath both these benches, and in the bushes. She's not around here."

Where are you, clever wolf? Markus asked.

Mischievous laughter rang in his head.

You can't hide from me, Markus reminded her.

No cheating, no, she snapped in return.

Markus tapped the scene sketches against his thigh. "Where did you start the game?"

"Just around that bend," Bella answered, pointing to the curve in the narrow path. "I stood there and she raced off."

Markus took a few steps forward and searched the foliage around the walkway. "How long did you wait?"

"I counted to thirty. I asked her how long, going up by increments of ten, she barked at thirty seconds." She wrapped her hand around the leather strap of her bag crossing over torso. "I have to say having a conversation with a dog was interesting."

Markus arched a brow.

Bella laughed. "Okay, so it's normal for you, but for us common folks, it's an experience." She shook her head, continuing to smile. "I'm still amazed she understood me."

"She told me I cannot cheat by using our bond to find her. So," he drew out the word and turned in a circle, "I will find her another way."

"Good luck."

"No luck," Markus said, creeping in a slow approach toward the only tree with any girth and full enough leaves to hide a devious wolf. "Simple reasoning."

Bella followed close behind, kicking up bark with each step. "I'm telling you, I looked everywhere."

Markus held an arm out to halt her noisy strides. "Not everywhere." He stopped under the tree and looked up. Two golden eyes full of mirth stared down at him. Her bottom teeth were visible as she smiled. "And no cheating necessary."

Bella was supposed to find me, Bella.

Come on down. Markus stepped back and motioned to the ground. "We have an investigation to begin."

Bella straightened, her eyes widening. "What did you learn?"

"Is the records department still open?"

She looked at the darkening sky. "I doubt it. I can tell you how to get there in the morning."

"You can take me," he said.

Frowning, she shook her head. "You know I can't, I have to work." She held up a hand when he opened his mouth. "And no, there is no talking to Master Guardian Perrella this time. Your investigation has nothing to do with the SNID."

"Do you have rest days you can take?"

"Not paid. I do get rest days, but as a clerk, I have to take them without pay, and I can't afford to do that."

"I'll pay you any days you need to take," Markus said.

Bella looked away, pulling her bottom lip into her mouth. "I don't know."

"It's not my money, if that makes you feel better. Vanscoyn is paying me a healthy sum, and part of the funds are to cover any costs I incur during the investigation. I consider hiring you to be a necessary expense."

Indecision still filled her eyes.

Markus leaned close and whispered, "I'll double your current daily pay."

"I can only take a maximum of two weeks."

He held out his hand. "Deal."

Bella stared at his hand and then slowly raised her gaze. "Are you sure?"

Markus grasped her wrist and placed her palm against his. "I'm sure." He squeezed and waited for her to return the gesture.

Her fingers tightened around his hand. "I hope neither of us regret this."

GARLIC, onions, and tomatoes sautéing in oil wafted past Bella, making her lift her nose and inhale deep as she opened the door to the tiny house she shared with her mother, Madeleine. Behind her, Markus let loose a groan of appreciation.

"Is that you, Bella?" her mother's voice traveled the short distance from the main part of the house to the small entry way.

"Yes, I'm home," she called, leading Markus and Lunah past a coat closet, a shared bathroom, and her mother's bedroom. Markus paused to hang up his long jacket, while Bella continued with Lunah following. "And I brought company."

Madeleine glanced over her shoulder, surprise flaring in her golden-green eyes. "Markus has returned?"

Bella smiled and patted Lunah's head. "Markus and Lunah."

"You told me they were arriving today, I'd hoped to see him. Glad I prepared extra."

"Hello, Madeleine." Markus took the short steps to the single counter space that counted as their kitchen. He leaned in and kissed Madeleine's cheek. "It's good to see you."

Warmth spread across her mother's beautiful face. She patted Markus's cheek. "You too, dear man."

"No leaving for extra food this time." He lifted a wax-lined paper sack, shaking it gently before setting it on their modest, round dining table. "Lunah has a bone for dinner, and whatever you're cooking will be a hundred times better than anything I've eaten on the journey here."

"Oh no." Madeleine frowned. "You didn't have a good voyage?"

Markus rolled up his sleeves, exposing forearms thick with muscle, emphasized by the leather bands around his wrists. "The ocean behaved, the weather as well. The cook I think lied on his application."

Bella turned to keep from staring at him as he made himself comfortable in her home. She pulled the strap of her bag over her head and went to her bedroom, only a few feet from where her mother cooked. At a little over five-hundred-square-feet, rooms weren't separated by much in their home.

"You didn't say you were hungry," she said, tossing her bag onto her narrow bed. Her jacket followed.

"Too many other..." His voice faded and Bella looked over her shoulder to find him studying the walls around her room. Wonder filled his eyes and slackened his jaw. His focus found her and she flushed under his questioning gaze.

She licked her bottom lip. Nervous flutters danced in her stomach. How to answer him without revealing too much? For five months he'd sent her letters. Beautiful glimpses into him as a man. The pages read more like a diary rather than impersonal correspondences. He'd bared his frustrations, hopes, and moments of happiness. Could she really offer him less in her answer?

Each letter had included detailed drawings of his house, his property, his favorite places to visit, or take Lunah hiking. Even though everything was black and white, the splendor of Ruthenia hadn't been lost. A land so different from hers, with soaring mountains visible almost everywhere one looked, cascading waterfalls, and at the time of the drawing, lush plant life taking advantage of the short, temperate months. In contrast, aside from the Tabria Mountains cutting through Sziveria to the north, and the cliffs to the south overlooking the Sovereign Channel, Sziveria was flat, with lots of fields dotted by woods and cut through by creeks. Pretty in its own way, but unexciting.

"I wanted to be where you were," she said

quiet enough to keep her mother from over-hearing.

Unmistakable desire darkened his golden eyes. Bella knew without a doubt he wanted to kiss her. Her heart did a slow turn, and she knew she couldn't hide the response to his longing in her own gaze. Why had she kissed him? If she hadn't jumped on him like a long-lost lover, then explored the depths of his mouth, neither of them would know what they were missing. Clasping his hands behind his back, he took a ragged breath and turned to-ward the drawings.

"Which is your favorite?" he asked, walking along the wall in slow steps.

Madeleine's laughter spilled through the open doorway. Lunah made happy noises. For the first time ever, Bella longed for privacy. She looked over the drawings, her attention lin-gering on the one she dared not mention as her personal favorite. The location of all her secret fantasies concerning the man who currently took up most of the available space in her closet-sized room.

Whoever had drawn the picture had pre-served the room exactly as they'd entered. An unmade bed against the far wall. A discarded shirt on the floor. A dog bed in the corner with a stuffed rabbit missing an ear. Curtains half open. Clutter took up every inch of space on the chest dresser. Paintings of ruins in a foreign land hung on three of the four walls. Markus's bedroom was such a personal space it was easy to imagine him walking through shirtless, or draped in a towel, his hair loose and wet around his shoulders. Late at night, it was just as easy to imagine she had the right to pull that towel free and....

Her imagination would get a little gray at that point. Aside from literature, and the collection of a pre-cataclysm artist, who's provocative sketches of sexuality had been recovered and were housed at the Sziverian National Art Museum, Bella had no idea what happened between willing partners.

She'd made the very personal choice not to settle for anything less than a relationship built on respect and love, which meant a marriage contract for longer than the minimum year. Bella didn't want a man in her bed who wanted nothing more than to forget her after a year and find someone new. She wanted it all. And after her mother retired for the night, she'd let herself imagine she had what she craved. Losing herself in Markus's world, and eventually in her yearning, when she finally stopped at his room.

No, she could *not* tell him all that. Mortification burned her cheeks at the thought. Even though she knew every picture by memory, she still looked them over. She pointed to a winding trail ending in a waterfall with a deep pool at the bottom. In the drawing, Lunah played in the shallow shore, her form mid leap, water droplets spraying from her fur.

"I love seeing her like this. Happy, youthful," Bella said, her fingers brushing the bottom edge of the sketch. "I wish whoever you asked to draw had captured you, too."

"My cousin did all of them for me," he said. "She took pity on me. Two years ago, she met a Cairoen Sentinel."

"I'm not sure what that is," Bella admitted, while inside relief filled her at knowing someone in his family had documented his life in pictures.

"You know of Cairo?"

"A brief mention from academia," she replied.

He rubbed the back of his neck. "How to explain this.... Education in Cairo isn't free, but it is required. If a family can't afford the fees, then when their children are finished, they owe Cairo so many years. The amount varies on the skills learned. Cairo then allows others, in their country or the inhabited world, to hire the skills they require. It's all highly regulated for the protection of their people, but still, in the end, a form of indentured servitude. The Sentinels are unique in that a family can give their sons to Cairo, where they'll be trained up into Cairo's elite fighting force. The Sentinels protect all of Cairo, and they can be hired as well. A Sentinel earns their freedom, though many choose to stay since it's the only life they've ever known. They can't marry or have a family."

Bella contemplated all he'd said. "If they

can't marry and have a family, how do they keep their military strength?"

"As I said, families can give their sons, and so can other nations, just as anyone can arrive in Cairo to learn a skill. They'll owe time, but they'll have the knowledge to take with them when their owed time is complete. And I didn't say they couldn't be intimate, though it's discouraged for the obvious reasons. One HRS incident could take out a lot of Sentinels before the infected is handled."

"And your cousin fell in love with a Sentinel?"

Markus nodded. "The ultimate forbidden love. Ruthenian's are discouraged from mating outside our nation, and he couldn't be with Mira until his time was complete, anyway."

Bella's heart clenched. "You can't take a wife outside of Ruthenia?"

His gaze met hers for a long moment. "I can."

An odd niggle twisted in her belly. There was more he hadn't said. "But?"

He returned to studying the images. "I'd have to move to wherever my wife lived. Our children would never be accepted as Ruthenian."

Our children echoed in her mind. "They'd forsake the next generation because they aren't pure?"

"*Dak*," he said without hesitation. "Genetically common offspring don't happen in my country."

"I remember you telling me that."

"They'd never be accepted. It's easier to simply leave, which many have done. The emergence of Gen-Heirs outside of my country prove Ruthenian's have left our island for generations."

"That's sad," Bella said. She tried not to think too hard about what his nation's prejudice meant for their future. Her dreams were just that, imaginations that would never go anywhere. She had even less to offer him than someone who at least had some measure of Ruthenian heritage running through their veins. "You'll never have new blood."

"We're a healthy population, though I will admit, the last two generations have struggled to have more than a single child. In time, Ruthenia may have to reevaluate."

Bella looked at the drawings Mira had taken the time to create for her. "Is your cousin waiting for her Sentinel?"

"I don't know. My uncle, her father, has attempted to find her a mate in Ruthenia, but she won't even consider anyone else, so maybe. She hasn't moved to Cairo, so I'm unsure of her plans."

"I can't imagine leaving your country, and culture, is an easy thing to consider," Bella mused.

Markus looked around her tiny room and Bella followed his gaze. Her bed, a single size mattress, was pushed against the wall into the corner. A small chest took up another corner.

She'd removed everything else to be able to walk unimpeded while touching the sketches he'd sent. All the wall space within touching height was covered in Markus's life, where she could visit whenever she had a free moment.

"I think," he whispered, "what could be gained would be worth more than what would be lost. The hardest part would be the risk of not knowing. Mira is scared to leave what she knows for something she doesn't. Perhaps, if her Sentinel could persuade her, she'd take the chance."

Bella pressed her lips together and took a bracing breath through her nose. "Would you need such convincing?"

He laughed. "Absolutely not." His eyes softened as he brushed a knuckle under her chin and along her jaw. "However, I have a suspicious feeling you would."

Bella was saved from answering by Madeleine's call to come to the table. Bowls filled with potato and cheese dumplings smothered in a garlic onion tomato sauce were already sitting at their seats. In a moment of great optimism, Madeleine had purchased a third seat for their round dining table over the summer. She'd patted the chair and said she had a feeling it would be useful soon. Markus noticed the chair and beamed at Madeleine. Her mother returned his grin.

Lunah chomped on her bone in front of the fire. Bella had found a thick wool rug on her walk home from a used mercantile shop. Like her mother, she'd held onto optimism the wolfdog and her master would return to their home. Even if the hope cost her disappointment in the long term. Bella pushed her dumplings around with her fork and wondered how she was going to get through the next two weeks with her heart intact.

THE CROWD PARTED in a wave of murmurs and exclamations of shock for Lunah. Bella walked a few steps behind the massive silver wolf, Markus at her side. Looking over at him, she wondered if maybe the lines weren't dispersing due to the beast master's dominating presence. With his braided wine-red hair falling halfway down his back, and leather coat swirling around his knees, he looked imposing, like a warrior of old.

"Is this normal for you?" she asked on the way to the clerks stationed behind the counter at the records department.

"Only here," he replied.

They stopped at the counter and Bella checked to make sure no one would demand their rightful place at the front. People stood a good eight feet from them, reforming lines at the other available clerks. She motioned for Markus to approach the man waiting.

"I need the public file for the Linettie Vanscoyn death record," Markus requested.

"Date of filing," the young clerk asked, his

expression and tone bored as he pulled a note card forward.

Markus frowned and dug around inside his jacket. He pulled out his notebook and read off a date. The clerk scribbled on the card and then with a sigh, rose and headed into the depths of file-filled shelves.

Bella turned and leaned back against the counter. "What are you hoping to find?"

"I'm not sure. I want the file before I ask you to look at the scene sketches."

All night, insecurities had kept her awake. In the morning, exhausted and convinced she'd ruin his chance of solving a possible crime, she'd been on her way to work and found Markus waiting for her on the steps. He didn't give her the chance to back out of their deal. Expecting her apprehension, he'd spoken to the master guardian over the Haven City division of the SNID. He'd held out the authorization for two weeks of unpaid rest days and then asked to be taken to the records department.

So here she stood, despite being unqualified, assisting a talented man in his search for answers. She could tell him, again, she didn't have a clue what she was doing, or how to really help him. He wouldn't listen, just like he didn't last time.

Lunah nudged at her fingers, her nose slipping under Bella's hand. Smiling, Bella followed the indent between Lunah's eyes up to the top of her head. She repeated the process when the wolf insisted. Her nerves soothed by the gentle petting, she smiled at Lunah's happy gaze.

"Thank you," she whispered.

"She asked when you'll realize how important you are, and not to worry," Markus said quietly.

Bella patted between Lunah's ears, unsure how to respond. Arguing with him would be pointless. He saw in her something she didn't understand, and couldn't see in herself. He'd tried his best to explain, to convince her of the talent he truly believed she possessed, but since she wasn't a genetic heir, she couldn't possibly be what he thought.

"Here's a copy of the HCES file included in the death record for Linettie Vanscoyn," the clerk intoned.

Markus accepted the thin folder, tucking it under his arm. "I have the scene sketches at Nick's. We'll go there, and Lunah can run the greenhouse while we work."

Five months ago, going to the Arch Guardian Wolvenguard's house had been nerve wracking for Bella. Unlike the other powerful arch guardians, Nick hadn't risen to power on ambition and politicking. His beast master talent alone had placed him within the rank, where the only person he ever had to answer to was the queen elect. While he could have allowed a certain arrogance to cloud his personality, she'd been surprised by his kindness and genuine good nature when she'd run into him a few weeks after Markus had left. Bella had a suspicious feeling Markus had asked the arch guardian to look after her in his absence.

They took a hired carriage to the Arch District, where the driver let them out at the corner. No one except those who lived, or worked, on the block of the six most powerful people in the country ventured onto the dead-end street. An odd quirk the city had developed over the years.

Lunah jumped around them, ran ahead, and then returned to start the process over. Her happy yips joined the songs of birds and rustle of leaves in the wind. Markus laughed. "She's pleased you're with us."

Bella smiled, surprised that even though she didn't know what she was supposed to do, she was glad to be with them. "I am, too."

Silence filled the arch guardian's monolithic house, the creak of the door closing behind them the only noise. Well, and to Bella's amusement, the squeak of her shoes and click of Lunah's claws. Markus, as usual, made not a sound. They headed past the impressive, wide stairs that split into two arching lines at the second floor to continue on to the third, several rooms Bella had no idea what they were for, and into what she figured was a training room. The left corner of the three-story-tall room was made of glass. One wall looked out into the conservatory, the other the rest of the property. A climbing wall reached to the ceiling in the center of the room.

Lunah ran ahead and out the already open doors into the greenhouse. In a flash, she disappeared into the thick, overgrown foliage. Padded couches were situated around a low, rectangular garden table. Markus had scattered colored pencils, notes, and the sketches across the surface. She sat on the longest couch, smiling when Markus joined her, their thighs nearly touching.

He tossed the file onto the table before removing his jacket. After rolling his sleeves halfway up his forearms, he retrieved the folder and relaxed back into the plush cushions with a groan. "Let's find out what the investigator believed he'd seen."

"Did anything in your conversation make you think there was definitely more going on than an accidental death?" she asked.

"*Dak.* He said he'd seen sleep aid in a medicine bottle on her nightstand, which is why he decided she'd fallen asleep and drowned, but he didn't note it in his report." Pages rustled as he flipped through them. "And I'm not seeing any mention of sleep aid in the medical science investigators findings, either."

Bella scooted closer and leaned into his arm to see the reports. She ignored the little thrill at being near enough to feel the heat of his body through his shirt, and smell his forest after rain scent. "Then why did they still say accidental?"

"The medical science investigator said she agreed with Key Guardian Prine's assessment, that the subject had been overly exhausted after a long voyage, became too relaxed in the lavender scented water, fell asleep and drowned," he read from the sheet.

"Was an autopsy done?"

He flipped through several pages. "I don't see one."

Bella considered all she knew about investigations and frowned. "That's odd. They must have really been convinced her death had no reason for suspicion."

Markus read in silence for a few more moments before setting the pages aside. "All right, let's see what you find in the scene."

Bella took a deep breath and straightened. Nervous flutters danced in her belly. She knew what she found, even if it was nothing, would be important to him. She waited while he laid the three sketches side by side in front of her so she could easily touch them. Clearing her mind and closing her eyes, she reached out and pressed her fingers onto the first sheet.

When she opened her eyes in her mind, she stood within the sketch. A world of black and white, done in hard uneven lines, and soft smudged shadows surrounded her. Nude, Linettie floated face-up in the tub, her hair suspended in tendrils around her shoulders.

"What do you want me to look for?" Bella asked, sliding her fingers to the other images. The room around her expanded to include a more detailed visual of Linettie and her bathroom.

"Anything that seems off, or out of place," he replied, his voice drifting around her.

"Right," Bella muttered to herself. Carefully, she looked over the room, from what the scene artist had captured around the tub, to the counter space, to the contents on the shelves. "I don't see any sleeping aids. I do see the lavender oil she used, and some bath salts."

"Ah, on the counter by the sink," he said.

Bella kept scrutinizing the scene. She stopped at the towels. "Well, that's odd."

"What have you noticed?" Interest sharpened his voice.

"There are four hand-towels, three washcloths, and only one towel." Bella looked around the room as preserved at the time of Linettie's death. "I see a washcloth folded by the soap in the corner of the tub, but I don't see any towels laying around, or even hanging for her use."

Fabric rustled, and not for the first time, Bella wished she had duality where her odd skill was concerned. She could hear the world beyond, but she could only see within the art.

"The washcloth looks to be wet, too."

In her mind, Bella stepped closer to the tub. A dry washcloth had a fluff to it. The artist had captured a flat washcloth, still folded, the corners off set from each other as if they'd slid some. "I think you're right. Not necessarily odd, except it doesn't appear to have been used."

"So, if she didn't use it, why is it wet?" he asked.

"And where are the other towels?"

Papers fluttered. "I don't see any mention in the reports of any towels being found in the bedroom."

"They may not have found discarded towels in the bedroom to be something notable, since she was in the bath," Bella said.

"Except, she's dead in said bath. I think towels on the floor in her bedroom would have been something they'd have been curious about."

"So," Bella said slowly, "the missing towels may be in the dirty laundry or were being laundered."

"Laundered wouldn't have anything to do with our scene. The dirty laundry however, might."

Bella removed her fingers from the paper, her awareness returning to the greenhouse. "Why?"

His intense golden eyes met hers. "Because, if someone killed her, they cleaned up after themselves, and deposited the evidence in the hamper on their way out."

FOUR

"Thank you for letting us in here," Markus said, pushing the door all the way open to Linettie's bathroom.

"Of course," Banks replied. "You have access to the entire house and all our staff, if necessary."

Markus's attention went to the towel shelf positioned beside the tub. "Would she have had all her towels the day she died?"

"Yes. Laundry is done daily. And since she hadn't been home to use any, all her linens would have been clean."

"Thank you," Markus said. "I'll let you know if we find anything or have additional questions."

Banks nodded and left them alone. A quiet sense of sadness permeated the room at his departure. Bella stood outside the bathroom, peering in.

"What are you hoping to find?" she asked.

"It's been weeks. Any evidence would have been cleaned away."

"Maybe," Markus agreed. "However, I don't believe in the perfect crime. Which means, if she was murdered, her killer left something behind. I intend to find out what."

Markus had toyed with bringing Lunah. But in the end decided any scent left behind by the potential murderer would have been too faint for her to detect. And that was only if she could find a matching scent somewhere investigators and household staff wouldn't normally venture, to discount them. His wolf was happy playing in the greenhouse, providing he returned to get her if they went anywhere afterward.

Bella hovered outside the doorway while he did a slow walk around the spacious bathroom. All the towels were exactly where he expected. He touched the fluffy linens and frowned in thought. "Will you look around her bedside table for any sleep aids?"

"Sure," Bella answered.

Markus searched around the bathroom. He found the usual bath salts and oils in the drawers, and a handful of cosmetics and feminine items in the cabinet. Molded floral hand soaps with dried bits of flowers filled a bowl next to the sink. Curious, he picked one up and sniffed. His nose wrinkled at the pungent rose scent. Tossing it back into the bowl, he wiped his fingers on his pants.

"Find anything?" he called.

"No," Bella answered, frustrated. "There's nothing except an unstrung ovulation bracelet, lotion, a few pamphlets from theater shows, and a..." Her voice faded and she cleared her throat. "A book."

Markus stuck his head out of the door. "Like a diary?"

Pink tinged her cheeks. "No, a reading book."

Markus tapped at the frame in thought. "Okay, normal bedside things, but nothing to help her sleep."

Bella placed the paperback book into the drawer and pushed it closed. "Not medicine, anyway."

Markus raised a brow. "What else is there?"

She continued to stare at the bedside table, a thoughtful expression pinching her face. He waited, and she shook her head, snapping from her revere. "Oh, nothing."

"Do you see the clothes basket?" he asked, looking around the spacious room.

A pink, sheer canopy draped over the large bed. A chest covered with a floral pattern pad on top sat at the foot. An armoire with a matching wood dresser and four-tiered book-shelf took up two walls. Woven rugs with flowers woven along the edges were laid over plush cream carpet. Paintings of castles with flowering vines added whimsy.

Bella pointed. "There, next to you."

Markus looked to his left. Outside the door, a pink wicker basket with a lid offered convenience to place dirty linens and clothes from the bathroom or the bedroom. He flipped the top up, not surprised to find it empty inside. The hinges creaked as the lid snapped closed. He leaned against the doorframe, the edge of the open door pressing into his back. Contemplating, he looked from the tub, back out into the bedroom, and returned to the tub. The scene flashed through his mind. Linettie floating lifeless in the water, the missing towels and mysterious wet washcloth. Crossing his arms, he walked to the bath. Muted light from a high window shone into the polished porcelain.

"What are you thinking?" Bella asked from the door.

"I do agree with the assessment that she fell asleep, but not that her death was accidental. I believe someone took her by surprise and held her under the water before she could fully realize what was happening. She struggled, sloshing water, but not enough to leave any marks, making it easy for someone to wipe up the evidence and leave," he surmised.

"Someone she knew?"

"That I don't know," he admitted. "If not someone in the house, then someone who broke in."

"Between her parents and the staff, someone would have noticed."

Markus shook his finger at her in thought. "Not if they snuck in and out."

Bella moved as he strode from the bathroom to the set of windows next to the bed. Squatting, he inspected the windowsill and locks. A hairline crack in the bottom left pane caught his attention. "Look here."

She joined him, leaning over and tucking an errant curl behind her ear. "What?"

"See this crack? There's still the mark from the heel of someone's hand." He pointed to where the light caught a smudge above the fractured glass. Rising, he opened the window and looked out. A tile covered awning from the first story balcony was positioned a few feet from the ledge. Satisfaction filled him. "Someone slipped on the roof."

Bella opened the second window and leaned out, gasping. "On all that moss. How did anyone miss that? It's a perfect slide, I bet they even fell on their butt and maybe went off the roof."

"No, look, whoever it was caught themselves, disrupting more moss, but the slide stops. The gutter is slightly moved from the edge, though. I bet that's where they went down to the ground."

Bella went back into the room. "So, someone came in through her unlocked window, found her asleep in the tub and took advantage, even cleaned up after when they realized it could look like an accident."

"Which is what happened. No one suspected murder."

Bella audibly swallowed. "What do we do?"

Markus closed the window. "We find the killer."

BELLA FLIPPED another page in Linettie's scrapbook, a collection Markus had called an 'I'm Important' book. Leaflets from every performance she'd been billed in, a ticket from each showing, newspaper articles and reviews were taped onto black paper pages, along with artist sketches of her performing on various stages in big, elaborate gowns. The assortment built a full image of Linettie Vanscoyn's life up until her death, starting at the innocent young age of fourteen. Bella couldn't imagine having to stand in front of strangers and be expected to perform, but Linettie had not only done so, but thrived.

"Look at her," Bella said, pointing to a colored drawing of Linettie in an emerald green dress. The artist had captured the subtle glimmer of detailed beadwork along the bodice and hem of the gown. "She's stunning."

Sitting next to her on the couch in front of the fireplace at her tiny house, Markus looked over from the box of important belongings Banks had handed over the second Markus relayed his suspicions. He spared the drawing a fleeting glance and a shrug. "You're prettier."

Bella stared at the blonde in the picture. Linettie's breasts spilled over the top of a cinched bodice and the flare of her round hips were accented by the cut of a gown meant to emphasis every full curve. Blue-eyes twinkled with the same glimmer as the beads shimmering in the light. A fine-bonded face captured in the full emotional delivery of whatever lyric she'd sent into the audience. Bella figured if the artist had captured the spectators instead of the artist, she'd be looking at lust and longing from the crowd.

"Are we seeing the same drawing?" she asked, flipping the page over.

"*Dak.*" He crossed his arms and rested them on the box, his gaze meeting hers. He flicked a finger at the picture. "Do you know what I see?"

She shook her head.

"A woman who knew she was beautiful and used it to her every advantage. From how her hair was styled to add height, to her gown, which drew the eye of every person she stood in front of, to her makeup, heavily applied to hide any imperfection. She was a carefully created façade I doubt anyone really knew, and she wanted it that way. Linettie was a rising star, a mysterious, stunning songbird everyone wanted to know more about. From the articles written about her, she never gave personal information, dropping hints that if anyone wanted to know the *real* Linettie, they needed to see her perform, for she was her voice." Shaking his head and sighing, he reached back into the box. "The real Linettie was sadly the one floating in a tub, without her gowns and perfect face."

Bella carefully placed the picture back into the book. "How sad. I hope her parents knew her."

"Maybe, at one time. Her career likely changed her, some. But, regardless, she was their daughter, they loved her, and she's gone from them now." He removed a small booklet, thumbing through the pages, and sighed again. Frustration tightened his face. "Everything personal in this box pertains to her career. There are no letters from lovers. No cards or mementos of friendships."

Bella turned another page. "What about booking agents, or a manager? A woman with her aspirations had to have had them, right? I mean, even painters have someone to help them organize galleries and exhibits."

"I'll send a message to her father asking for that information," Markus said, tossing the booklet back into the box. "She kept nothing from them if she had support staff, though."

Bella considered the very personal objects among what little she'd found in the singer's nightstand. "I don't think she had a lover, but I think she was considering taking one. I don't believe she'd promised to contract with anyone, that would surely have been in one of the many articles and her parents would have known. But someone had caught her attention enough for her to purchase an ovulation bracelet. She hadn't strung it yet, so she wasn't tracking her cycle, but maybe someone had made her believe a promise would be coming soon, or she'd decided to chance an unmarried relationship."

Markus set the box on the floor and then leaned back on the couch, rubbing his forehead. "Except her father didn't mention anyone in her life."

Bella turned another page, scrutinizing the preserved articles and sketches. "Okay, maybe a secret romance?"

He rested his head all the way back and stared up at the ceiling. "Those do have a habit of going wrong."

The end of the collection revealed nothing more than a woman infatuated with her rising fame. Bella snapped the book closed. "She *must* have had friends. Someone she knew and confided in, someone we can talk to who can tell us who may have been a potential rival, or lover."

Markus rolled his head to look at her. "I'll ask her father about that, too. I'm not holding out much hope though, since he didn't mention anyone we could speak to aside from the household staff."

Bella pulled the box closer and rummaged around inside. Two red bound books rubber banded together caught her attention. "What are these?"

"Lyrics," he answered, dropping an arm over his eyes.

Bella unwound the band and opened the top book. Neat, loopy cursive greeted her. Lines of poetry ran the length of each page. Excitement filled her and she had to fight to keep from grinning. *Finally*, something personal to Linettie. She set the journals in her lap and picked up another small paper booklet from inside the box. She flipped through the pages.

"This is a music book." Holding the book open to a center page, she turned it toward him. "See? Song title, the year it was written, the key it's supposed to be sang in. Didn't you take music in early academia?"

He stared at her for a silent moment. "No."

Bella flipped the pages back around. "I bet you can sing well. You have a nice voice."

"*Dak*, nice enough to scare children," he said dryly. "The singing is more Lunah's gift."

She laughed. "All right, fair enough." Bella tossed the lyric booklet back into the box and handed him one of the red journals. "This isn't a lyric book, but it's poetry that she wrote. Maybe we'll get lucky and she mentions someone by name."

Markus sat up. "I thought it was a lyric journal. My sister kept them. She wrote all the words down from her favorite performances so she could sing them afterward."

"But I bet she titled the songs, like in the music book." Bella tapped at the top of the page she'd opened to. "These are only dated."

Markus turned through several pages. "Damn. You're right." He nudged her knee with his. "Now do you believe me?"

Bella nibbled on her bottom lip. "You would have figured it out, eventually. I didn't do anything special."

She realized her mistake a second too late. Before she could even squeak, he'd hauled her to straddle his lap, his mouth covering hers. The journal tumbled between them to fall on the couch, bouncing closed. With the tip of his tongue, he slipped between her lips, coaxing her mouth open for him to explore. And explore he did. Kissing, and kissing, and *kissing* her until she thought her heart would burst from the thrill of his mouth moving over hers.

The room titled. Though he never stopped the seductive assault on her senses, she somehow wound up under him, pinned to the aging couch cushions. The delicious pressure of his body over hers did funny things to her inside. Flutters danced low in her stomach, winding downward to settle in a curious throbbing at her core. Bella couldn't help bending her knees to cradle his hips. He groaned, and deepened his kiss. The sound sent a new wave of tremors through her.

Markus ground against her, leaving no doubts that he was as excited as her. The hard length of him rubbed just the right spot to steal her breath, sending a sharp arc of pleasure through her. Bella's eyes flew open and she stared at the ceiling. Needing something to hold onto when his hips dipped again, she clutched at his shoulders.

"Oh wow," she breathed, unable to stop a moan when he pressed harder, longer. "Wow."

"I need…" Another harsh groan left him and cold air brushed her stomach. The tips of his fingers touched her trembling abdomen. Little electrical snaps danced across her skin. Bella arched into the caress. His breath, hot and fast, moved across her cheek. He muttered words she didn't understand. "I need to touch you."

Bella blinked in confusion. "You are touching me."

"No." His tongue licked a sultry path along her jaw to the pulse-point in her throat.

Bella turned her head to give him better access, her fingers moving to sink into his soft hair, wishing it were unbound. His touch moved along her stomach to her hip, tracing the curve and causing her to squirm. When he moved to the waist of her pants, she realized what he meant by *touch*. Anticipation and alarm made her still.

Markus rose above her, his gaze heavy and dark with longing. Slowly, he eased his fingers beneath the band. Bella wanted to tell him to hurry, or maybe stop, because should they be doing this?

No, definitely hurry.

An ache she knew only he could satisfy thrummed at her center. Except, what happened next? They hadn't discussed the future, if they could even have one. Which Bella knew was unlikely.

So what?

Why did she care?

This was Markus. *Her* Markus, even if only in her mind. If he were to be a first in sensual experiences for her, would she ever regret it?

He sighed. His hand returned to her hip, while his forehead dropped to hers.

"Why did you stop?" Bella asked, puzzled.

"You are overthinking again," he whispered against her mouth. He pressed a gentle, tender kiss to her mouth. "Someday, you will be too lost in passion to think."

Heat flamed her cheeks and she squeezed her eyes closed. "Sorry. I just..." His words registered and her eyes flew open to stare at him again. "Someday?"

He caressed her cheek, his smile warm, showing the hint of dimples she knew appeared when he grinned. "I hope for there to be many such moments between us."

"But—"

"Bella, darling, are you home yet? I was thinking sautéed herb beans in garlic with fried cheese bread for dinner tonight," Madeleine's voice funneled through the small entry into the living area. Metal hangers clinked together. "Bella?"

They moved at the same time. Markus scrambled off her as she scurried out from under him. His hair was an odd, lopsided mess and Bella snatched the band from the end of his braid. She made hurry motions, and he slid his fingers through the dark, glossy strands. Bella straightened her clothes and picked up the journal, opening it in her lap. Markus pulled his hair into a ponytail.

A sense of mischief made her press her kiss-swollen lips together to keep from smiling. Maybe they'd get lucky and her mother wouldn't look too closely at them. Despite being well into adulthood, there were still very adult moments Bella hadn't experienced yet. She'd never trusted a man enough to let him get to the point where something could happen.

"Oh!" Her mother stopped inside the small threshold, her hand to her chest. "Markus."

"Dinner sounded great," Markus said smiling, and braced an elbow on his knee to face Madeleine. "Though I might not be here." He tapped his head. "Lunah has begun to fuss. I won't be able to leave her alone much longer."

Madeleine set a canvas tote on the table. "You can come back. I'll be sure to make enough."

Markus turned his head to meet Bella's gaze. His hair slid over his shoulder. "Perhaps I will."

Bella's heart squeezed, hitching her breath. If her mother had waited longer to arrive, Bella would, at this very moment, likely be experiencing something wonderful. The heat reflected in Markus's gaze told her he was having the same provocative thoughts. Bella turned her attention back to the journal.

He leaned close and whispered, "Coward."

She clenched her jaw and glared at him. "My mother," she said between her teeth.

Markus kept his focus on Bella. "I kissed your daughter, Madeleine."

"About time," Madeleine chimed. "I'll be in the greenhouse if you need me."

Markus smiled. Bella snapped the journal closed and smacked his arm. "I can't believe you did that!"

"Your mother likes me. And if you think we fooled her, you're mistaken." He touched her chin, still tingling from their embrace. "You look thoroughly kissed, Bella." Leaning close, the tip of his tongue touched to her bottom lip, making her lean in close, eager for another kiss. Forgetting, that easy, her mother was only a few feet away, outside. "Another thing I plan to do again. Often."

ORANGE AND PINK streaked a sapphire sky, casting colorful rays onto the decrepit buildings lining a street so narrow carriages couldn't venture down. Known in Haven City as The Rows, only bikes, single rider carts and horses could navigate them. At his side, Lunah's silver fur took on the warm golden light. The beautiful sunset almost softened the harsh reality of walking past the homes of people too poor to fix a broken window, patch a roof, or replace a rotted board on a porch step.

Bella lived here, amongst the drudges of society, with the sex hustlers, and drug brokers. And while he knew this wasn't the worst part of town— that distinction was left to the off-limits section of the Old City Ruins— it was bad enough to make him uncomfortable when he left her. The chilly breeze, ripe with the promise of oncoming winter, reminded him months would pass again when he returned to Ruthenia before he'd see her.

Frozen water, and later ice drifts, made nautical travel impossible in the winter months. Crossing the formed icefield held its own impossible dangers. Ruthenia was unique, in that when the artic winds blew down, they became completely separated from the rest of the inhabited world. In the past, this had been what his ancestors coveted. The isolationist attitude meant finding a mate from another country was, while not outright forbidden, frowned upon to such a degree all who found love beyond their shores, left. Markus shoved his hands deep into his pockets. Contemplating the difficult future he may face if Bella turned out to be his mate, brought anxiety he wasn't ready for yet.

But that kiss. This was the second time she had ignited in his arms. Markus had never experienced such raw passion. He wanted more. He wanted all of her. Months ago, Bella had made it clear she wasn't interested in anything except forever. A long-term marriage contract. The longer he spent around her, the more he discovered the incredible woman she was, the more certain he became he'd give up what he knew for the unknown future at her side. Before any of those thoughts could be entertained, however, he had to help her understand what life with a beast master entailed. She may run in horror once she knew...

Lunah sensed his unease and nudged his arm. *She will accept us, she will.*

As you have accepted her? Markus dared to ask.

Lunah lifted her nose into the air, ears twitching. *She is yours, she is. I have accepted this, I have.*

She isn't mine. Not yet.

She cast him a sly, sideways glance. *Already started, the bond has already started.*

Markus halted. He stared at his wolf. She stopped steps ahead of him in the center of the uneven, broken brick sidewalk. "What?"

Her golden eyes twinkled. *The first thread has been woven, the first.*

Markus pressed a hand to his chest and searched inside. He recalled the moment he'd touched Bella's bare skin while he'd kissed her. The tiny arcs of sensation that had sizzled across his fingertips. Something he didn't remember happening during his previous moments of intimacy. Was that a bond forming? He figured he'd always know when it happened, so he'd never bothered to ask his parents, or other beast masters, what to expect.

You can feel it? The bond? he asked.

I am sharing the bond with another, I am, she said.

Markus needed to sit. He plopped down right there, among the broken bricks and dirt. "I thought..." He swallowed against the sudden dryness coating his throat. "This doesn't make any sense. I've only kissed her."

Lunah pressed her damp nose into his neck and licked his bearded jaw, her attempt at offering comfort. *She must be different, she must.*

Markus wrapped an arm under her neck and patted the side of her face. "I suppose we figured that out months ago."

She yipped in agreement.

The soft whir and tick of a bicyclist speeding by joined the distant echo of a dog barking and a woman shouting indiscernible words. Another, louder female voice lifted on the faint breeze. Paper fluttered by, swirling with dead leaves. Markus breathed in the not unpleasant scent of someone's dinner cooking. Lunah bumped her side into his shoulder.

"All right," he sighed, and stood with a groan.

Lunah urged him to move, pressing her nose into the back of his leg. Markus laughed, and ruffled the fur between her ears. "I'm moving, wolf."

Move faster, I want to see Bella, move faster.

They walked several rows until they

reached Bella's house. A lantern burned at the front door, illuminating the sagging steps in the dying light. The door swung open before he could raise his hand to knock. Bella smiled and beckoned them to enter. Markus couldn't help leaning down and kissing her lips as he walked by. The moment was so domestic, and comfortable, he could imagine doing the same routine for decades. Lunah licked at her fingers and insisted on being petted, rubbing her head under Bella's hand.

The scent of garlic, pepper, and bread filled the small house. Markus's stomach grumbled. Lunah had eaten before they left the arch guardians. Madeleine set two plates on the table. Her dark brown hair streaked with a hint of gray fell in a long braid to her hips. She smiled, reaching across the short distance for a basket of toasted bread slices.

"I'm glad you came back to eat with us," Madeleine said.

Markus took a seat at the small, round table. Bella sat and Lunah curled at her feet. Too big to fully fit, the wolfs fluffy tail swept back and forth between their chairs. They ate along with companionable conversation. Markus pretended not to notice Bella sneaking Lunah small pieces of bread under the table. Lunah, being a good dog, took the pieces with a soft mouth, but was unable to stop the snuffling chomp of delight.

Between bits of conversation and bites of his food, he tried to focus on the thread Lunah claimed had developed between him and Bella. If his wolf could sense it, shouldn't he able to as well? Perhaps his attraction was so strong, it felt like the start of a bond. Despite months of correspondence, and a passionate greeting, they hadn't discussed any sort of future. Markus wouldn't, no *couldn't,* take away her choice. If she said no to a life with him, he'd have to respect that, bond or no bond. In Ruthenia, any relationship he started began with the intention of forever if a bond formed. Sziverian's didn't. They entered into a trial run, and after a year, decided if they wanted longer. Bella's desire for a longer relationship may be tested when she realized he meant forever. Literally. Once bonded, there would be no one else for him.

Markus realized with a shocking sense of dismay, he couldn't allow the bond to grow further, not without her permission.

Madeleine paused with her fork halfway to her mouth. Frowning, she set the food down. "Is everything all right?"

Markus snapped from his depressing thoughts. He forced a smile. "*Dak,* fine."

She patted his knee under the table. "It'll all work out."

"I did find some poetry entry's you might be able to get some clues from," Bella offered, spooning the bean mixture onto a slice of toast.

Markus met Madeleine's gaze. Understanding shone in her golden-green eyes. He could, right this moment, tell Bella what really caused his distress. Instead, he took a long drink of cool water, and nodded. He didn't want her mother included in certain parts of the conversation. Things about him Bella needed to know, that as her mother, would likely not be appreciated.

"I can't wait to see," he said.

Lunah nipped at his ankle. *Tell her, tell.*

I will, when we have privacy.

A snorting exhale sounded under the table. Markus rubbed his boot between Lunah's shoulders. After dinner, Markus helped Madeleine with the dishes, while Bella and Lunah went to do the chores in the small, porch greenhouse. The routine was one they'd fallen into months ago, when he'd been visiting.

"You're going to have to tell her," Madeleine said, handing him a dish dripping with clear water.

Markus accepted the dish in a towel and carefully dried the clay plate. "I know."

Madeleine looked at him sideways from beneath long lashes. "You aren't surprised I know?"

Markus set the dish on an open shelf to his left. "No. I'm sure your talent allows you to see many things."

"It does," she agreed. "But not all things. Do you love her, or is it only knowing she could be a potential bond-mate that has you pursuing her?"

Markus braced a palm on the counter and

regarded her. "There is no potential, Madeleine," he said softly. "Not anymore."

Some color left her caramel skin. "I see. I thought, perhaps, you were only considering. I hadn't realized…"

Markus took a plate from the rinse water. "I hadn't either. Lunah did."

She took a deep breath and continued washing. "Do you love her, then? Is love even necessary?"

"I don't know," he said, answering both her questions at once.

Madeleine touched a wet hand to his wrist. "I know you'll be good for her, and the bond means you'll never stray. Love…" She shrugged. "It'll come when it's meant to."

Markus shoved thoughts of love, and bonds, and complicated futures from his mind. "The next couple days might be late for her."

"I know. I'm glad you convinced her to work with you. She's so talented, I wish she could see that."

"She will."

Moist, warm air swept into the room ahead of Bella and Lunah. Water glistened from Lunah's muzzle. Dirt smudged Bella's arms, darkened under her nails, and streaked across the bridge of her nose and along her jaw. Her ocean-green eyes met his, such a contrast to her pale brown skin and dark hair, he was again rendered breathless by her beauty. Errant curls framed her face, the rest of the mass she'd piled atop her head in a messy collection that worked for her.

"Five of the pepper seedlings were ready to be transplanted," Bella said, showing off her messy hands. "I think the rest will be ready in a day or two," Bella continued.

Madeleine stepped away from the sink, drying her hands. "Are there enough pots?"

"I'll get a few more when we're out tomorrow." Bella washed her hands.

Markus liked the *we* part of her sentence. He handed her the towel he'd been using. She accepted with a smile. Lunah slipped into Bella's room. Before Markus could ask what the wolf thought she was doing, out loud or through their bond, a loud *bang* sounded from the front of the house. Madeleine spun around, her hand on her chest. Bella grabbed a skillet.

Two men sauntered into the small living space, coming to stand on the rug between the couch and fireplace. A burly man with a shaved head and dark mustache stood a step behind a small, wiry man who became Tiny in Markus's mind. Glasses perched from the end of Tiny's beak-like nose. Gray-hazel eyes looked over Bella from behind the round frames. Tiny's attention flickered between Bella and Markus. He licked his thin lips.

"Well, well, if I'd known you Fenwick women were *entertaining*, I'd have found an agreeable amount to help pay down your debt," he said, his voice a harsh whisper.

An orange scarf wrapped around his neck

and draped down his chest, hiding what was likely an old throat wound accounting for his raspy sound. He glanced at the couch, and with a long exhale, settled onto the cushions. His arms spread wide, as did his legs, and he surveyed Bella again. The lust-filled glint in his eyes made Markus clench his fist behind his back.

Tiny motioned with his fingers in a *let's go* motion. "I'll wait, go on, finish with your current client."

No one moved. The small iron skillet in Bella's hand didn't even twitch. Markus kept himself very still, fighting the urge to launch himself at Tiny. Who was this guy and what right did he have to walk into the house as if it were his? Markus knew nothing about their landlord. Perhaps the scum sitting on their couch owned the home.

Madeleine recovered first. Her spine straightened and a smile that didn't reach her eyes curled her mouth. "Mr. Hossman, what an unexpected surprise." She motioned to Markus. "You misunderstand the situation. This is Mr. Ralston, he's visiting from Ruthenia."

Markus angled his body and grasped Bella's free hand, which happened to be her left. Carefully, he slipped one of his bracers free and wound it around her wrist. She looked over her shoulder at him, incredulous. He gave a light shake of his head, a motion only she would notice.

Hossman smirked, his body becoming even more relaxed. "Even the foreigners know where to find the best romp."

"I would suggest," Markus said slowly, "that you stop speaking about my promised in such a fashion."

To her credit, Bella didn't turn around and start arguing with him. Though the sudden stiffening of her posture told him she wanted to. She set the skillet on the counter and took a step back, to his side. She didn't reach for his hand though, understanding he needed to keep them free. He did reach out and brush her arm. A quick contact that went a long way to soothe his nerves.

Hossman slouched further on the couch and gave a derisive sniff. "Whatever makes you feel better about giving in to her hustle." His beady eyes slid over both the women again. He reached crudely between his legs and adjusted himself. "If I'd known, I'd have been the first in line, too."

Markus didn't hesitate. *Lunah, strivhat.* And then as a quick afterthought, as his wolf sprang from the doorway behind him, he added, *Zo nieho kuya'te.*

Hossman's shrill scream echoed around the room the second Lunah latched onto his balls.

You owe me for this, you owe me, she said, her thoughts strained. *Gross, so gross.*

Hossman attempted to move, and she growled. Face splotched and red, sweat streaming from his temples and arms raised, the tiny man breathed in sharp gasps. Baldy shifted, a subtle movement, and Markus leapt over the table, unsheathing a knife he kept strapped at the small of his back.

"Touch her, and you die," he whispered, his voice thick with his accent. The tip of the blade scratched at stubble on the underside of Baldy's chin. The man lifted his head, both hands raised, just like his boss. "Good choice."

Markus kept the blade trained and Lunah remained fixed on her target. *Back off, slowly.*

Lunah eased away, releasing her hold. She remained in an aggressive stance, ready to lunge back into action if Markus required it of her, ears back, teeth bared.

"Here's how this is going to work," Markus began, "are you both listening?" He waited until they both nodded. "You're going to walk out of this house, and you aren't going to return."

"That's kinda hard to do," Hossman stammered. "Y'see they owe me."

Markus narrowed his gaze. "Owe you?"

"Yeah. Raimarks. Lots of them."

"Define lots."

Hossman rattled off a number. Markus did the conversion in his head and almost choked. The amount *was* a lot, but not more than he could afford. However, one look at Bella and he knew she'd never allow him to pay her debt. Everything came together in perfect clarity. Her fear over losing her job. Why she lived in a hovel, in a risky part of the city.

"Have any of her payments been late?" Markus asked.

Hossman shook his head. "No."

"Then why are you here?"

Hossman licked his thin lips, his attention skittering from Lunah to the women and back. "I heard... a rumor."

Markus waited.

"That Bel... uh, Miss Ralston, lost her job at the SNID."

"So, you come here, and disrespect her by treating her like a sex-hustler?" Markus asked, the tip of his knife edging into Baldy's skin. The man made an uncomfortable noise. Markus ignored him.

Hossman's hands trembled, from the effort to keep them raised, or from fear. Perhaps both. Markus didn't care. "I apologize." Light flashed from his glasses when he turned his head. "To you both. I'm sorry. Very sorry. Deeply sorry."

Markus eased the knife away and took a step back. "Don't let it happen again."

Hossman jumped from the couch. "Nope. Never." He swallowed, the sound echoing in the small space. "Regular payment schedule, delivered to my office."

"Of course," Madeleine said. "We haven't forgotten the stipulations, Mr. Hossman."

"Good, that's uh," he glanced at Markus, swallowed again, cleared his throat, and continued, "that's good."

The two men hurried from the living room,

Hossman clutching the front of his pants. Markus tilted his chin upward when Lunah glanced at him. *Follow them out.* Lunah obeyed, disappearing behind them into the small entry.

Madeleine turned away, but not before he caught the shaky rise of her hand to her mouth. She faced the counter, her hands braced on the surface. Markus returned his knife to the sheath while crossing the short space. He touched a hand to Madeleine's stiff shoulder.

"It's okay," he whispered, "they're gone."

Madeleine nodded. "I know, I just..." She took a long, uneven breath. "He showed up here and would have made demands we couldn't meet, I know it. And then..." She shook her head again.

And then he'd have made an even greater demand that two women alone wouldn't have been able to fend off. The knowledge made him want to return to when Lunah had the man's balls between her teeth and have her finish the job.

"Does he have a habit of rape?" Markus asked outright, not caring if it was vulgar.

Bella stepped behind her mother and rubbed her upper arms. "I don't know about rape, but he does have a reputation for requesting sexual favor in return for payment. Male, female, it doesn't matter to him."

Markus raised his brows. "That's a great risk."

"Yes. I always watch them both closely

when they show up for signs of rabies infection."

Madeleine sniffled. "Your father was ignorant of Hossman's methods, or he never—"

"You don't know that," Bella snapped and stepped away. Anger reddened her cheeks and shone in her eyes. "Papa wasn't thinking at all when he borrowed those raimarks. If he had been, he never would have taken them in the first place."

"You know—"

Bella slashed a hand through the air, cutting off her mother's words. "Yes, I know what he *thought* he was doing. And he died anyway, didn't he? And we lost everything, thanks to his ill-conceived plan."

Bella opened her mouth and then closed it just as quickly. Tears shone in her eyes. She shook her head, waved in dismissal, and turned, disappearing into her room. Lunah reappeared, glancing at Markus before following behind Bella.

Madeleine sighed and placed her back to the counter, gripping the edge. "I'm sorry. Obviously, this is still an unhappy topic for us."

"I doubt losing him will ever be a pleasant one to discuss," Markus said gently.

Madeleine shook her head again and looked over the small living area. "No. He became really sick, and we didn't have the money to pay a Gen-Heir Medical Scientist to learn exactly what was going wrong. An academia trained MS told us it was likely incurable anyway, but Davis, he was convinced if he could learn exactly what was wrong, they'd be able to fix him. When he came up with the money, I didn't question it. I should have, but I didn't." A tear raced down her cheek and she swept it away. "I wanted him fixed too, you know?"

Markus nodded but said nothing.

"Anyway, the appointment was made, but he died before. The money we had left I used to pay our bills since Davis hadn't been able to work for months. When Mr. Hossman came calling for his money, I realized what my husband had done. We had to sell the house, but even that wasn't enough. My other two children couldn't help either, so..."

"Bella took a job with the SNID, and you both moved to the rows more affordable housing," Markus guessed.

She nodded. "Yes. I took a job as well, and began charging for my counseling and matchmaking sessions."

"You still owe a lot."

"At his interest rate, we may never pay him back," she whispered.

"I could—"

"No," Madeleine rushed out. "We are not your responsibility." He opened his mouth, and she held up a hand. "I know you think otherwise, and I understand. Perhaps I should say Davis Fenwick's debt is not yours to handle."

Fair enough. "Your other two children?"

"Have families of their own. When Lemar and Junie didn't even help us move, Bella had a fit on them both and refused to leave me to handle this on my own. She still doesn't speak to either of them. Not that they ever come visit. I refuse to be an unknown in my grandchildren's lives, so I do go to them, but, it's been hard on Bella. All around."

Davis Fenwick had not only left his wife in trouble, but had torn his family apart over the massive debt he left behind. Bella's fury toward her deceased father made perfect sense. Markus stepped to the right, closer to Bella's room, and leaned over to peek through her door. She lay curled around Lunah on her bed. Markus's heart clenched. The house was so small, she'd probably heard every word of the conversation. Bella looked her young twenty-three years, and vulnerable, wrapped around his wolf like she was a giant stuffed animal.

Madeleine excused herself and went to her room, giving the illusion of privacy the thin walls would never manage. Markus shifted to Bella's door, leaning on the jamb, arms crossed.

"You must think we're pathetic," Bella's said, voice muffled by Lunah's fur.

"No, but I do think you're in trouble. Hossman is not a good man, and no one on this street will care if he returns."

She turned her head enough for her beautiful eyes to meet his. "I know what you're thinking."

Markus raised a brow and waited.

"You can't stay here. We can't afford for a

man to be seen leaving this house in the morning that isn't married to one of us," she said.

Sighing, Markus tilted his head back and stared at the water-stained ceiling. "All right. Will you let Lunah stay?"

Lunah lifted her head, her golden eyes penetrating.

Will you stay if I ask it of you, and Bella allows? Markus questioned.

Yes, I will, yes.

Bella sat up enough to scoot against her modest headboard. Her hands stayed buried in Lunah's fur. "Can she be away from you for that long?"

Markus shifted, uncomfortable. He didn't like the thought of leaving this house without both of them. "You could come with me, to Nick's. Both you and your mother."

She'd started shaking her head before he even finished.

"No?"

"No. I'm sorry... I can't stay at the arch guardians."

"Well, you could."

"I'm a—" Her mouth snapped shut when he cast her a warning glare. A flush spread across her cheeks and he knew she was remembering what happened not so long ago when she'd put herself down. "It is not done for someone outside of the arch guardian's staff, or social class, to stay in his home. People talk, and not well. I work among too many people who are aware of the gossip surrounding ranked guardians, and my mother and I staying in his home would definitely cause gossip."

"Then I guess we'll learn how long Lunah and I can be separated."

CHAPTER

FIVE

Bella awoke to a warm, furry body squished against hers, and the alluring scent of coffee. Her mother never made coffee, she said it upset her stomach first thing in the morning. Which meant... Bella sat up with a gasp. Lunah raised her head, unconcerned, licked at Bella's chin and laid back down. If the wolf wasn't worried, then Bella likely didn't need to be either. The urge to lay back down and bury her head under the pillow tugged at her hard. Somehow, she made herself ease from bed, reaching for a wrap hanging from the post of her headboard.

Glass tinkered and something jangled. Bella tied the sash around her waist and stumbled into the moderately brighter living area. The lack of windows and other houses built so close kept their home in a perpetual state of gloom.

A fire burned low in the hearth. Markus's large frame shuffled around her tiny kitchen, from the small cast-iron pot he'd heated in the fire and used to brew the coffee, to a cutting board with colorful fruit half-sliced. Seeing him in her space, waking up with him *here*, did funny things to her stomach. He stuck his finger into the pot, hissed and pulled it free, shaking pale brown liquid off.

"Didn't your mother teach you not to touch hot things?" Bella asked, yawning. She covered her mouth and went to the nearest seat. "How did you get in?"

He dug into his pocket and produced a shiny silver key. "Madeleine gave me this last night."

"Ah." Bella glanced at her room. "Why didn't Lunah warn me?"

"She knew it was me, and greeted me at the door." He cast her a fleeting smile before turning his back to her. A knife blade pounded a rhythmic beat.

Bella stared back at her room. "I didn't even notice."

Markus shrugged. "Predators are usually known for their stealth."

The predator in question appeared from the darkness, her bright, golden eyes seeming to glow before the rest of her materialized in the doorframe. Bella blinked. "Is that coffee ready yet?"

"Almost."

A bowl of diced fruit landed in front of her, followed by a rolled paper bag of cinnamon-sugared oats and a jar of heavy cream. Bella's mouth watered. "I haven't had these in... a long time."

"Mmm," he hummed. "After what I learned yesterday, I figured your diet is mostly broth and beans."

Bella pulled the oats closer. The scent of sweet spices swirled around her. "We eat better than that with our little greenhouse, which we're very fortunate to have."

Markus placed two steaming cups of coffee on the table and then took a seat across from her. He motioned at the oats. "Go ahead, you don't have to wait on me."

Smiling, Bella shook a heaping pile of oats onto her fruit. She poured thick cream into the bowl and into her coffee. Markus did the same. Lunah curled up in front of the fire. Halfway through their breakfast, Markus set a folded piece of paper on the table.

"Banks sent a reply to our inquiries, it arrived before sunrise," he said.

Bella set her spoon down and opened the folded slip. She read over the note. "A few close friends from academia, but no one she still communicated with after she began her tours," Bella muttered to herself. "She did have a manager."

"And a booking agent," Markus said, tapping the paper where a name was underlined. "The manager handled her daily life, while—"

"The agent handled her career." Bella blew out a puff of air and slid the letter back to him. "She must have been doing pretty well to afford paying two people to travel with her."

"They're both from Haven City, I've already researched their addresses. I figured we'd start with them, see what they can tell us, and if they know of anyone else involved in her life."

Bella tapped her spoon against the inside of her bowl in thought. "I wonder if one of them will be who she'd chosen to be a lover."

Markus took a heaping bite of oats and fruit. Cream drippled from his spoon. He waited until he finished before speaking. "I imagine traveling everywhere together, romances do form in those situations."

"And they're both men," Bella noted, rising with her now empty bowl. She rinsed and set it in the sink.

Markus looked her over, his gaze lingering on her very exposed legs. "Go get dressed."

The heat in his eyes matched the bloom of heat across her cheeks. Bella ducked into her room, his laughter chasing behind her. She closed the door and leaned against it, waiting for the wild beat of her heart to return to normal. Feeling in the pitch dark, she found the matches she kept on a small shelf beside the door and lit the lamp. Light burst into her small space. She went to the small chest beside her bed and dug around inside for something nice.

When she'd started at the SNID, Madeleine had gone through her closet and given Bella all the clothing she no longer wore. The clothes were a bit big, since her mother was fuller figured, but much nicer than anything Bella had owned. She found a loose pair of teal silk palazzo pants, the flared legs looking more like a long skirt than pants, and paired it with a plain cream long sleeved shirt, and a bright, floral princess vest.

Winding a lime knit scarf around her throat, she opened the door, ready to face the day helping Markus investigate. At least, that's what she told herself, because really, she'd just be there for... what, she wasn't sure. Moral support? Not that the intelligent man surveying her from in front of the fire needed his hand held. Maybe for *her* morale. She loosened the scarf from her skin and reached for the messenger bag slung over the back of the chair.

Lunah stood, heaving a long, loud yawn, licked her upper lips and then sat, tongue hanging out. Bella adjusted the bag over her chest. "Do you think it's wise to take her?"

Markus slid his fingers between Lunah's ears. "She won't go without me today."

Confused, Bella looked between them. "Why?"

"Because we were apart last night. She did well, but she won't leave my side today."

The urge to go to him, to touch him in comfort, shocked her. She grabbed the strap of her bag. "How did you do?"

"I wanted to be here. With both of you," he said without hesitation. "I didn't sleep well."

"I'm sorry."

He offered a half smile. "Me too, since I know it's going to be the rest of my stay in Sziveria."

Bella chewed on her bottom lip. "We're fine, you know."

"No," he said, shaking his head. "I don't know. Which is the problem." He rubbed a hand down his face, sighing. "I'll figure something out."

Bella went to argue, but he didn't give her the chance, walking past and out of the room with Lunah trotting after. Her fluffy tail swept back and forth in a cheery rhythm. Bella grabbed a coat from the closet, shrugging it on as she followed them outside. Cold air slapped her. Ice glistened on the uneven brick road, and the roofs of the houses lining the street. Smoke puffed from chimneys and woodstove pipes, filling the air with the haze and scent of burning wood. She squinted against the sun glimmering over the tops of the houses across from her, right into her eyes.

Markus waited for her a few houses down. The bright light brought out the dark, rich red of his hair, hanging in a braid over his shoulder. She really, *really* wanted to feel his hair loose beneath her fingers while he kissed her the way he had yesterday. There were a lot of areas on the man she wanted to feel beneath her fingers. Swallowing against the sudden dryness of her throat, she made sure the door was locked and then shoved her hands into her jacket pockets and met him down the sidewalk.

At the corner of the street, they flagged down a hired carriage. Markus gave the driver the address and then climbed in behind Lunah. Bella braced herself as the carriage lurched into motion. The leather strap still tied around her wrist caught her by surprise. How could she have forgotten that, not even having noticed while she dressed? She went to remove it and Lunah's paw landed on her lap. Big golden eyes stared at her.

"Don't," Markus whispered.

Bella met his gaze and shifted her focus back to Lunah. "Don't what?"

"Remove my bracer. If Hossman comes around again, he needs to believe what I told him."

"But—"

Markus shook his head. "No. It may keep him away, for now. Please, leave it on."

Bella eased her hand away, her fingertips lingering on the stiff leather before falling to her lap. "All right."

He blew out a long exhale. "Thank you."

They rode in silence, the awakening city passing by the small windows. Shopkeepers switched tin signs to open. Vendors set up their carts of goods, from food to scarves, hoping to eek out as many sales as possible before the artic winds kept everyone indoors. Between Wintervail and the promise of months without being able to venture for necessities, vending always increased before winter. Bella mentally catalogued what their home still needed before the ice and snow arrived. Glass jarred food, firewood, another rug if she could manage, a few herb plants to make the jarred food more palatable to consume.

Lost in her inner list making, she missed Markus's words. The deep rumble of his voice tugged her from her thoughts. She shifted her attention to him. "What did you say?"

His face twisted in exasperation. She stifled laughter, wondering if he only expressed his emotions so vividly around her. He laid his head back and stared at the roof. The long lines of his neck beckoned to her. In a flush of awareness, she wanted to close the distance between them, climb onto his lap, inhale his scent, and then taste the strong cords at his throat. Lunah whined and settled onto the floor, her head on her paws. Bella snapped from her fantasy.

"Why were you nervous yesterday? On the couch when I wanted to touch you?" he finally answered, or rather repeated what she hadn't heard.

Bella's stomach clenched. Could he ask a more personal question? She worked her jaw, returning to watching the city pass by. "I wasn't nervous, just cautious."

In her peripheral, he raised his head, his piercing golden stare narrowing. "Oh? Cautious of what?"

Bella considered her answer and how much

to reveal. She liked this man. A lot. Her attraction to him surpassed any she'd felt for men previous. Not that she'd found many men appealing. Most were lazy, lust-driven, or unwilling to commit for longer than the required year for contracts. None had ever made her wonder if longer than a year would be worth attempting. The result had been a few quick kisses, maybe a groping of her breast or two, but nothing so intimate as touching her skin underneath her clothing. Looking over the masculine specimen sitting across from her, Bella knew, without a doubt, once he touched her, she wouldn't want him to stop. And that scared the courage out of her.

"I don't know what you want from me. What you expect." She took a bracing breath. "No one has ever... I haven't... I'm, um, very much..."

"Inexperienced?" he offered.

Cheeks burning with embarrassment, she nodded.

He leaned across the distance and took both her hands. "How inexperienced?"

Bella stared at their joined hands. The silver rings on both his hands stood out against the deep caramel of his skin, a contrast to her own pale brown. Not darker. Different. A tantalizing glimpse of how his body would look pressed to hers with nothing between them. "I hadn't even kissed anyone seriously, before you."

Her confession shocked him. The surprise

morphed into something she couldn't quite recognize. He brought her knuckles to his mouth, rubbing them back and forth before kissing them. A quiver danced in her stomach at the tickling sensation of his beard and the satin softness of his lips.

"I will never expect more than you're willing to give. As for what I want..." His gaze darkened as he looked her over. "I think I've made that very obvious."

The harsh beauty of his accent thickened with his words. Tremors flipped through her lower belly. "All of me, or just my body?"

"You are part of your body, Bella," he whispered, his breath hot across the back of her hand.

"That's not an answer." She lifted a finger, brushing the bristles of his trimmed beard.

He pulled on her hand until she leaned closer to him. Close enough to breathe in his rain-drenched forest scent. He was silent for a long moment. Only the rocking of the carriage and clatter of wheels and hooves on brick filled the space. Bella wondered what he had to say to her and why he wanted her near.

"In Ruthenia," he began, his touch a maddening feather along her throat, jaw, and collarbone. A constant flutter of sensation. "When we find a potential mate, if our wolves get along, we sequester ourselves at an isolated location. We quarantine for two weeks, as a precaution meant to satisfy that we're both healthy."

Bella was sure she wouldn't like what he was about to say. The only reason to quarantine would be to ensure neither had become infected with human rabies syndrome before engaging in a sexual encounter. She steeled herself against rising jealousy.

"Afterward, we mate, to see if a bond forms."

"Mate?" she asked, and yep, there was the jealousy turning into a giant stone in the pit of her stomach. "As in...?" She waved a hand, unable to say the word.

He grabbed her hand, lacing their fingers together. "*Dak.*"

Wariness filled her. Bella yanked her hand free and tried to sit back, away from him. "There will be no *mating* between us."

"I know." He maintained a tight hold on her wrist to keep her in place. "I told you for two reasons. One, so you would know I am not inexperienced. It seemed fair to share that part of myself when you had. Two, so you understand I'm in unfamiliar territory. Beast masters don't court in my country. If we're compatible, a bond will form after a physical relationship. At least... that's what we've always been led to believe."

"What do you mean?"

He inhaled to speak when the carriage lurched to a stop. Bella would have flown across and into him if he hadn't reacted, bracing his hands on her shoulders, keeping her in place. Lunah rolled onto her side, into the siding of the seat. A second later, the driver pounded on the roof and announced they'd arrived at their destination. Lunah rose, gave a full body shake, ready to exit first. Markus leaned forward to open the door and then helped Bella stand. Pedestrians exclaimed in surprise the moment Lunah leapt free and landed on the sidewalk. A man with a paper brandished it like a shield, edging away. He slipped on the curb, catching himself from falling at the last moment. Bella rolled her eyes, jumping from the vehicle. Lunah came to her side, a happy smile on her face, her tongue hanging between her two bottom canines.

"She's pleased to be with us," Bella said as Markus disembarked beside her.

"*Dak*, very much." He ruffled the thicker fur at the back of her neck. Shading his eyes from the streams of brilliant sun glaring between the buildings, he surveyed their surroundings. "I think... this way."

He turned to the right and headed down the sidewalk. Lunah fell in step behind Bella. Markus stopped at a three-story structure. The residential apartment building had an occupants list posted beside the door. He ran his index finger down the list, tapping halfway down. Questions unrelated to the case swirled in her mind. She wanted to finish their conversation. A glutton for heartache, she also wanted to know more about his attempts to find a mate.

Markus hefted a thick wooden door open.

Warm, dry air rushed past them. He held the door for her and Lunah, following behind them into a shadowy stairwell with a hall to the bottom level apartments. At least, she figured that's what the four doors, barely visible in the narrow, unlit passage, led to. Markus brushed past her, his big hand gripping the wooden rail to the stairs as he climbed upward. Bella followed, Lunah at her heels. She managed to make it to the third-floor landing before she couldn't stand the anxiety any longer.

Bella grabbed the tail of his jacket before he could take another stair. "Wait."

He paused, his foot raised. "*Dak?*"

She licked her lips and turned to face the narrow window overlooking an alley below, the only source of light in the switch backing stairwell. "Did you love any of the women you..." She swallowed against the hard lump in her throat. She could do this. Ask the impossibly personal question. "You mated with?"

"No," he answered, his voice a quiet whisper behind her.

Air lodged in her throat. Dismay warred with elation. "How could you give them your body if you didn't?"

"Bella." He urged her to face him. The silvery light from the window cast across the planes of his face. He brushed a touch across her jaw, to her throat. "Our ways are not the same. I know you don't understand, that you may never understand. Though I know many here enter into a short-term, safe relationship, without any love, and none ever forms. As a beast master, when I find my true mate, a link will form between us. Usually, a physical relationship will trigger the link. Love often follows. How can it not when we're bound together in so many ways, for the rest of our lives? But at the start? No, there is no love. There may not even be lust, just a sense of duty to discover if we share the potential to bond."

She searched his eyes. "How many times have you tried?"

His gaze narrowed. "Are you sure you want the answer to that? Does it really matter?"

Bella pondered his question. Would a number change anything, except make her feel worse? She blew out air and shook her head. "No, it doesn't matter."

But what did that mean for them? The future seemed the one conversation neither of them could bring themselves to start. In a strange stairwell wasn't the place, either.

He tucked hair behind her ear and then squeezed her shoulder. "Okay?"

Taking another cleansing breath, she nodded. "Yes."

"I didn't tell you any of that to upset you."

"I know." She grabbed his forearm and returned the squeeze of reassurance.

He searched her face for another moment before heading up the stairs. "The apartment is on the fourth floor, almost there."

Lunah raced ahead before Markus took another step. Markus's jacket swished around his knees with each step, adding a whisper of sound to his otherwise silent ascent. Even Lunah, a true predator, made little scratches of sound with her nails on the wooden steps. Bella scrunched her nose at each echoing clomp of her boots following behind them.

"If you continue to insist I keep working with you," Bella said, her grip tight on the outside rail, "you're going to need to teach me this floating on air thing you do."

He laughed and glanced over his shoulder at her. "The what thing I do?"

She waved at his booted feet. Boots that should weigh more than hers based on their sheer size alone. "You don't make a single sound when you walk. How?"

"If your quarry hears you coming, you aren't much of a surprise, are you?" he answered. "Silent walking is something beast masters learn from the moment we start taking our first steps. Our parents teach us. More often than not, our assignments are dangerous, stealth may be the difference between success or death."

"We aren't sneaking up on criminals or opponents," she felt the need to point out.

He shrugged, stepping from the landing into the short corridor that led to the apartments on the floor. "It's part of me now, how I always walk, or even run."

Bella had to work hard not to get stuck imagining him dashing from tree to tree, a soundless wraith pursuing a target, his long, dark hair and jacket trailing behind him. "Can you teach me?"

Each door they passed had small wooden numbers nailed beside the frame. Markus stopped at 4-3. "I don't know, but if it's important to you, I could try."

"I don't like sounding like a herd of cows chasing after you," she admitted.

"You're not loud."

She raised a brow in disagreement and he chuckled. The dimples in his cheeks deepened. Summer sun, how she loved it when he smiled.

"All right, fine," he said, "you're louder than me, but you aren't a herd of hooves loud."

She motioned to Lunah. "I'll settle for being wolf loud."

His smile turned lopsided. "Wolf loud, huh? Lofty goal, but we'll try."

Before she could answer, he knocked, reminding her they weren't hanging out in a hall to chat, but for a purpose. She shoved her hands into her jacket pockets, hating the sense of displacement. Of knowing, again, she didn't belong with him on an investigation. The door swung open and a man with dark hair hanging down into eyes stared at them.

"May I help you?" he asked, securing a cloth belt around his waist to keep the long, black satin robe he wore closed.

Markus stepped to the side so the man could see Bella, and Lunah at her side. "I'm Markus Ralston, this is my wolf Lunah, and my... assistant, Bella. We're here from the

Vanscoyn's, about their daughter's death. May we come in?"

The man looked them over and then stepped to the side, his face pulled in a frown. "Yes, sure, please. Has something changed? I thought her death was an accident."

"I'm investigating for them as requested," Markus answered.

"Right, of course, I appreciate you taking on the case. Her death has been difficult for many of us," he said, closing the door. He fidgeted with the end of his belt and then motioned down the narrow corridor. "Would you like some tea? Juice?"

"We're fine, thank you. Do you have time for a few questions?"

"Yes." He led them down the hall. "We can sit in the living room."

The hall led to a quaint living space. A half wall separated the kitchen and dining rooms. Plants lined the divider and hung from the ceiling in front of every wide window. Knit blankets in earth tones draped over the couch and a reclining chair. Musical composition books and loose sheets of music littered the coffee table. The man brushed hair from his eyes as he sat in the recliner, gesturing for them to take the couch. Lunah walked to the window and looked out, her breath blooming vapor across the glass.

Markus pulled his notebook from inside his jacket. "Terran, correct?"

"Actually, I'm Orin. Terran is—"

"Who was at the door, babe?"

Orin lifted his hand on a smile as Terran strolled into the room from the hall, a towel draped low on his narrow hips. Water dripped down his neck to run along his pale chest and thin arms. He stopped short, his dark eyes growing wide.

"Oh, oops. Sorry." Terran took a hasty step back into the shelter of the dimmer corridor.

"This is Markus and Bella, they're here to ask some questions about Nettie. Why don't you get dressed and join us?" Orin suggested.

"Sure thing, I'll be out in a second."

WELL, that answered the question about whether Nettie could have been considering one of them to be her lover. Then again... "We were hoping you could answer some personal questions. Her parents didn't know of any friends she may have confided in. Since the two of you spent the most time with her, did she share anything private with you?"

Orin looked between the two of them, question clear in his rich brown gaze. "Such as?"

Markus glanced at Bella.

Thankfully, she understood his unspoken request. She licked her lips and rubbed her hands on her thighs. "Linettie had an unstrung ovulation bracelet in her bedside table. She wrote some pretty graphic poems in her lyric journal about a potential lover. Do you know who?"

"Nettie was very beautiful, and she caught the attention of many affluent men who hoped to enter into a, what are they calling them, shadow contracts? Exclusive affairs without the longer term, legal filing of a marriage contract. Of course, anyone who's willing to enter into relationship outside of a marriage contract is suspect in my opinion, I steered her away from such ventures. A diamond necklace wouldn't do her any good if she turned into a zombie because of an unfaithful scum bucket."

Markus made a note. "Did she turn anyone down here in Sziveria?"

Orin shook his head. "No. She had many offers in Westica and Monaco Sands. We'd only been home a day when she'd..." He swallowed and waved at his face, red with incoming tears. "I'm sorry, I thought I'd cried myself out over losing her."

"Take your time," Markus said softly.

A shaky breath left him, and he wiped his knuckles under his moist eyes. "I don't know of anyone here that had caught her interest. Then again, she seemed convinced anyone she took an interest in, Terran or I would as well."

"Did she have reason to?" Bella asked, her expression a mixture of innocent curiosity.

Orin laughed, sweeping hair from his forehead. "No, none at all. If a man was interested in Nettie, he wouldn't look *my* way, would he?"

"And Orin wouldn't do anything about it,

anyway," Terran said, sweeping into the room. He joined Orin on the chair, perching on the arm and draping his forearm on Orin's shoulder. "Right?"

Orin patted Terran's hand. "Right, which Nettie knew. We contracted within a month of Terran joining our little team. She had some insecurities where men were involved."

Markus looked up from his notes. "How so?"

"She was a late bloomer," Terran answered. "We were halfway through her tour of Westica before she'd wear a gown that showed any of her curves. Before that, she wore flowy fabrics that hid more than revealed, and not in a flattering way. She was convinced she didn't have anything anyone would want to look at."

Orin nodded. "Yes, but her first night of wearing a beautiful gown with a low neckline and hip hugging waist, she had people lining up to meet her. She couldn't believe the difference, all because of how elegant she looked. How her confidence changed, resulting in her appearing more professional on stage."

"It wasn't an overnight turn around," Terran said. "She still doubted herself."

Markus glanced sideways at Bella, understanding the frustration of dealing with such self-doubt. "Did any of her admirers seem like the type to have followed her home?"

Terran leaned back on the chair, his arm sliding along the back behind Orin. "They certainly all had the money to be able to chase after her, if they wished."

The cushions shifted slightly as Bella adjusted her position, her face drawn in thought. "If someone did, and they were keeping their affair a secret, how could we learn who he is?"

Terran rose from his perch on the chair arm and went to a small desk in front of one of the windows. He shuffled through papers and returned with a yellow sheet. "Here's a list of the all the men who showed an interest in a liaison with her. For most singers, the relationships last for the duration of their stay in whatever city they're performing in, and the expectation is she'll be shown complete lavishness during the terms of the shadow contract. Everything paid for, and daily gifts from her lover. She asked me to keep track of them, and write my impressions, should she ever decide to. We, of course, advised against such behavior. She was above being a paid companion."

"But the temptation was there?" Markus asked, accepting the paper.

Orin frowned and reached for Terran's hand when he neared. "Maybe. One man—"

"I circled his name," Terran said, pointing at the paper Markus held.

"She seemed to consider in Monaco Sands. We were going to return there after the winter thaw, so she had time to decide."

"And track her ovulation," Markus said. He slid the names into the back of his notebook after writing down the possible lover's name.

"Is there anyone else here in Sziveria she may have gone to see that we can ask about her personal or professional life?"

The men looked at each other. Various expressions and subtle body language passed between them. Orin snapped his finger, his eyes widening. "Her music instructor."

"Oh yes," Terran exclaimed. "Adelaine Waynick."

"She's *the* voice instructor for anyone hoping to have a professional career. The Vanscoyn's were very fortunate she accepted Nettie as a student from her audition," Orin said. "Nettie always went to see her after touring, to learn what she could have done better and to continue training her voice in her off time."

Markus stood. "Thank you both. We appreciate your time. If you think of anything else, send it to the Vanscoyn or Arch Guardian Wolvenguard's residence."

Terran's brows rose. "Arch guardian?"

Markus nodded, putting away his notebook. "It's where I'm staying."

They shook hands with the gentlemen and left. Lunah led the way back to the street. Instead of hopping into another carriage, Markus grasped Bella's hand and walked down the sidewalk, among the rush of city dwellers in a hurry to get to their destination. A wide berth extended out from them, courtesy of Lunah's dominating presence. Markus smiled to himself.

If only you received such respect in Ruthenia, he quipped to his wolf.

None of them would last in our lands, none of them, she said, a huff of annoyance snorting from her nose.

And yet you find my mate among them, he couldn't help but remind her.

She is not of them, she is not.

No, she isn't, he agreed, his fingers tightening around Bella's.

Bella looked at him, a curious smile playing on her full lips. Kissable lips. Markus focused on the sidewalk and not tripping over an uneven brick. He guided her to a small bakery he'd discovered that served hot filled pocket sandwiches. The dough crispy on the outside and the cheese and shredded ham he'd had a salty, savory delight. Delicious scents wafted past as he opened the door. Bella murmured her approval.

"Have you eaten here?" he asked.

"No. I don't get to eat from vendors much."

How could he forget? "Ah, sorry."

She shook her head. "It's not your fault."

Markus ordered, getting three extra's for Lunah. The baker handed over their food in paper sacks once they were finished. Outside, Markus asked, "Is there a park nearby, or a public greenhouse?"

Leaves skittered down the sidewalk and floated in the cool breeze swirling around them. Bella tucked an errant curl behind her ear, her nose scrunching in thought. He waited, rolling the tops of the bags to keep the contents warm while she glanced up and down the street.

"I don't know this part of the city very well," she admitted with an apologetic smile.

"All right, let's walk and see if we can find somewhere to sit and eat."

A few streets up they found a small park with a circular trail. Cement benches, black and green from weather and a fine coating of algae, were positioned every few feet. Bella sat without a second glance or concern. When he hesitated, she laughed.

"Don't tell me you're scared of a little dirt," she said, her voice as warm as the sparkle in her eyes.

Markus looked at the seat again and swept his coat up before sitting beside her. "This is a very expensive jacket."

"If only they could see the savage now, your reputation would be ruined," she teased, taking a paper bag from him.

Fragrant steam wafted from the sack. His stomach growled and he made quick work of putting Lunah through her sit and lay commands. She licked her muzzle and waited with patient anticipation glowing in her eyes as he held up the sandwiches. He laid them between her paws in a neat pile. Drool plopped on the ground next to the meal. She licked her muzzle again, but her eyes never left his. Markus held up a finger, a silent command to wait. He unwrapped his own sandwich, took a bite and then motioned for her to continue with her meal.

"What was that for?" Bella asked. The bag on her lap rustled.

"I'm alpha," he explained after he finished swallowing. "I always eat first if we're sharing a meal."

"I thought you were equal," she asked, tearing off a chunk of her sandwich instead of biting. Cheese oozed onto her fingers and she sucked them into her mouth. She pulled them free and repeated the process.

A visceral, very male reaction had him following her glistening fingers from the bread to her lips. "If you don't stop that woman, I won't be held accountable for what happens next," he growled.

She paused, a bite halfway to her mouth, eyes wide. Slow, and much neater than her other bites, she placed the food between her lips and chewed. Markus took a centering breath, urging the desire running like fire through his veins to dissipate. The middle of the park, in the harsh light of afternoon, was not the place to ravage the beautiful Sziverian.

"Perhaps I spoke too soon about that savage nature of yours," she whispered.

"Perhaps you did."

She used the bag to clean off bits of cheese. "You were explaining about your relationship to Lunah."

"Was I?"

"Yes."

What was it she'd asked? Or said? Markus glanced down at Lunah, finishing up the last of the pockets and tried to remember. Ah yes, his alpha status. "While we're bonded, we aren't necessarily equal. I'm still a man and she's still a beast. As a wolf, she requires certain etiquettes be met to make sure she's secure in her position at my side. If she loses confidence in me, in my ability to lead and care for her, she won't be able to function at her full potential."

"You cherish her so much I can't see her ever losing confidence in you."

"I wield a lot of power over her. The possibility of my allowing that authority to compromise us both is there. It's happened in the past, with other beast masters. Our routine helps remind me she's trusting in me to do the right thing, for us both."

Bella sat quiet for a moment, wiping crumbs and cheese from her fingers. "Is the bond with a mate the same as with Lunah?"

Markus fed the rest of his and Bella's food to Lunah, contemplating how to answer. The paper sacks crinkled between his fists as he balled them together. "For two beast masters, it's close. Each bond is different since each couple is unique, but over the years there are things that don't change between Ruthenian pairs. A heightened awareness of our mate. A man can tell when his wife is ovulating, which is helpful since it can take a year or longer to achieve conception."

Her cheeks pinkened, but she didn't shy

from the topic. "For Ruthenian's that marry outside of the nationality it can take over a year to conceive, too?"

He shook his head. "That I don't know, but I don't think so. Medical Science doesn't allow us to know for sure what's happening, but it's theorized that our women choose which genetic material passes to ensure a healthy pregnancy and a strong offspring. It may take months, or years, before her partner gives her material that is found to be acceptable. You..." He waved at her body. "Won't have that."

"But since you'll be able to tell when I'm ovulating, I could potentially get pregnant very easily," she said, more in thoughtfulness to herself than to him.

Still, Markus found himself choking on her reflection. At the knowledge she was considering, even if just for this second in time, a future with him. One that involved both of them naked and sweaty in the best possible way. "The first year or so, it'd be impossible for me to stay away from you," he agreed.

She took a deep breath. "I see. So, an ovulation bracelet..." He shook his head, and she mirrored the action. "Ah. I see."

"I mean, it could help to know when you'd have to kick me out of the house," he tried to joke.

She blinked and stood up. "Why are we even having this conversation? You aren't going to give up your country and I'm..." She cast him a sideways glance and shook her head again. "Were the two men telling the truth?"

Joining her, he tossed their trash into a nearby can and motioned for her to start walking. "Lunah didn't alert to any lies."

"How will you find out about the men who were interested in Nettie?"

Lunah did a full body shake before catching up to them. Markus held his hand out and she brushed her head underneath his fingertips. "I'll go to Immigration and Import and ask to see passenger manifests. They aren't private. I'll see if any names match. I'll ask her parents about the music teacher. Chances are they have all her information, and we can go visit her tonight or tomorrow morning."

"I wonder why Mr. Vanscoyn didn't mention her," Bella said.

"Maybe he didn't know Linettie still went to see her."

"How could he not? She was continuing to improve in her profession and was still living at home while in Sziveria, he must have known something of her daily affairs."

"Maybe, maybe not. Do you tell your mother everything *you* do every day?"

She flushed and shoved her hands into her jacket pockets. "No, of course not."

"From what we've learned of Linettie, I think she likely left the house when she felt like it and said nothing to either of them. After all, she'd been traveling the world without them, living her life without any permission as to what she could, or could not do," he said.

Leaves tumbled over their feet and swirled along the walkway. Branches rubbed and creaked above them, the last of their leaves shivering in the wind. Bella hunched deeper into her jacket and Markus resisted the urge to pull her into the warmth of his side. The promise of the arctic winds soon to arrive chilled the breeze. A hint of ice and the tang of rain. A reminder his time in Sziveria was running dangerously short.

SIX

The resonance of voices in perfect harmony filled the cavernous entry hall of Adelaine Waynick's home. Like an ocean wave, the sound crested and broke in the open space, leaving chills along Bella's arms. Beside her, Markus stood still, every limb taut, the muscles in his jaw jumping. He stared down the empty corridor, waiting, like her, for their host to finally greet them.

Bella occupied herself by easing along the wall covered in drawings and paintings of students and the performances of the instructor herself in her younger years. One striking image dominated the wall. Adelaine wore a gown with a royal blue crushed velvet bodice and peacock feather skirt that flowed from her hips and draped across the polished wooden stage. A crown of finely worked gold and peacock feathers sat atop her head. One hand pressed over her diaphragm, the other fisted with emotion, she delivered a performance worthy of being immortalized in paint.

The haunting howl of a wolf joined the rising pitch of the song. Shocked, Bella spun around and found Markus shaking his head, his hands over his eyes. He spread his fingers and peeked at her through the slits.

"I tried, she couldn't take it anymore," he said over the cacophony of sound. "She says the song of her kind is much better, she is proving it."

Lunah gave it her all, head back, muzzle forming an O, more of a prolonged, broken whine than musical notes leaving her. Bella laughed and shook her head. The wolf's tactic worked. A sharp, abrupt silence blanketed the house. Bella's ears rang at the loss of sound.

Heels clicked on the white marble floor. A tall, lithe woman emerged from the shadowy depths of the corridor. A regal maroon satin skirt swirled around her ankles and a fitted black top showed she took care of her figure, even in her advancing years. Head held high, her nose more predominant than in her painting, and hair in a severe bun without a strand out of place, she looked every inch the authoritarian instructor.

"Can I help you?" she asked in a tone that implied she'd rather they turn and walk back out her door than assist them in any capacity.

Lunah chuffed at her and sat. Markus sank his fingers into the fur between her ears. "We're sorry to interrupt," he began, "but we have some questions about Linettie Vanscoyn."

No emotion crossed the older woman's face. "She's dead."

"Yes," Markus said. "I'm investigating her death. We were told she came to see you on the day she passed, to continue her training."

Adelaine pressed the tips of her fingers together for several moments, her gaze considering. She popped her thumbnail and middle finger together and sighed. "Very well, in here if you please. I don't have much time, my students are waiting."

"Thank you."

They followed her into a cozy sitting room with four chairs arranged around a round table. A lilac and baby's-breath bouquet sat in the center. Leaflets from varying performances were arranged neatly on the table. Adelaine sat in a graceful motion, her spine straight. Bella found herself mimicking the posture, not wanting to feel like a slouch next to the woman.

"Nettie was a star pupil of mine. I was very proud of her. She had many plans for her future," Adelaine said, crossing her knees and folding her hands on her thigh.

Markus sat across from the teacher, taking out his notebook. "Did you ever discuss her personal life, or only her professional?"

"I was not here to be a confidant," Adelaine snapped. "I listened to her scale, we discussed where in her songs she felt she was losing strength and what she needed to do to improve. She was always a high achiever, she wanted to be the best someday. If she took any lovers, or met any instant friends, I know nothing of that."

"What about professional conversation? Did she ever seek advice on venues or singing for private events?" Markus asked.

Adelaine straightened her already rigid shoulders. "Of course, she did. I know everyone important in this industry. Some of them are predators, others will sink careers, or help float them into the clouds. My opinion matters a great deal to my students, Linettie included."

"Did you advise her to stay away from any venues or private interests at your meeting?"

"Not really. I did tell her she could do better than the house she booked for her second tour in Monaco Sands, and gave her the contact information for the owner of another establishment."

"Can I have that information?"

"Yes." She leaned over and pulled a fine cord behind a well-placed curtain. Seconds later, a young man rushed into the room. "Flynn, darling, will you please go into my office and get these people the contact sheet for that little concert hall in Monaco Sands."

His pale-brown gaze flickered around the room. "The Blue Space?"

Adelaine tsked and glared. "No, not that one. Ivory Notes Hall of Sound."

"Ah, yes." Red tipped his ears as he backed

out. "I'll be right back with that."

"Was she having any issues with competitors?" Bella asked while they waited.

"Competitors?" Adelaine raised a dark brow. "Darling girl, my students don't have competition. They are levels above anyone else out there."

"Any issues with other jealous singers?" Markus asked.

Adelaine wrinkled her nose and sniffed. "There will always be those envious of a talent they'll never hope to possess."

Bella wanted Adelaine to expound on the statement, but Markus caught her stare across the short distance. And in an instant, she knew what he wanted. *Wait.* Unspoken, yet understood between them. Quickly, she dropped her gaze to the table, looking over the programs from shows. They were all performances Adelaine had headlined. Bella searched through them, noting The Blue Space was one of the listings. Two other venues from Monaco Sands were spread on the table. Bella wished she had a notebook of her own, wanting to know more about the other establishments and unsure if she'd remember the names.

The quiet waiting finally paid off. Adelaine sighed. "There was one girl, Henley Jasper, a spiteful little thing. While I don't think she's of any concern if you're trying to learn more about Linettie for her parents to find closure, Henley *was* known to harass Linettie at local events when she was home. Parties where the host would convince Linettie to do an impromptu song, things of that nature. I refused Henley as a student five years ago, if that helps you understand her lack of talent."

Flynn returned, a sheet of paper flapping in his hand. He went to hand it to Adelaine, who gave him a withering stare and waved her hand at Markus. He changed course and offered the information to Markus. "I included three other venues she'd asked Mistress of Song Waynick about."

Laughter threatened to escape at Adelaine's ridiculous title, spoken by the young man with an air of reverence that made Adelaine's chin raise in superiority. Bella had heard of a Mistress of Etiquette, who taught young girls raised in ranked society how to behave, but not a Mistress of Song. She wondered if the title was self-appointed.

"Thank you," Markus said, folding the paper and tucking it into his notebook. He had quite a collection growing in the back of the thin book.

Adelaine stood and shook out her skirt. "I hope you learn whatever it is the Vanscoyn's were hoping to discover of their daughter. Her death was a loss to the music community."

Bella rose with Markus. Adelaine swept from the room, Flynn chasing behind her. The click of her heels faded, leaving them in silence. Markus reached down and picked up a program. He flipped it over, grazed the contents and then dropped it back to the table.

Bella handed him the two from Monaco Sands. "I think we should look into these along with the names she gave you."

He didn't question her request, simply wrote down the names. Doubt twisted through her and she almost asked him to stop.

"Whether we find anything or not, checking won't hurt anything," he said without looking up. "Don't think what you have to offer isn't an important contribution to the case."

The papers fluttered from his hand back to the table. He met her stare. "All right?"

She nodded. "All right."

Harmonized vocals rose. Lunah howled. Markus sighed. Bella threw her head back and laughed, wondering how she'd ever go back to her boring existence in a basement after they left her. Again.

"Thank you for waiting," Henley Jasper said as she swept into the room.

The sun streaming in the front windows highlighted her already brilliant red hair. A cream tunic shirt embroidered with gold thread, longer in the back, fluttered behind her over flowy black pants. A dusting of pink eyeshadow and thick line of kohl made her already vivid blue eyes shocking. She carried a manilla folder in her left hand. Her gaze never left Markus, a flirty smile teasing her full lips. Bella wanted to do something, anything, to assert a claim on the beast master she had no right to stake.

The strong floral notes of roses, patchouli and musk floated in the air around the woman. Bella's nose itched. Lunah outright sneezed, spraying dog snot on Henley's pants when she ventured close enough to reach a hand to Markus. Lunah sneezed again. Henley waivered in her attempt to reach out and took a few steps back, sitting across from them. Bella patted the wolf's head.

Henley glanced at her pant leg, offered them a weak smile, and set the folder on the table. "When Ms. Rosell said you were here regarding Linettie Vanscoyn, I went to get some research I've been doing for several years."

Markus picked up the folder and flipped it open. Bella had been expecting a collection of bad press reviews or negative gossip columns. Yes, the file was filled with articles, but on dead singers, not just Linettie. Markus picked up a clipping and laid the rest on Bella's lap.

"What is this?" he asked, frowning.

Henley patted her thigh, grimacing when she encountered a clump of Lunah slobber. She flicked her fingers in disgust. "Linettie wasn't the first singer to die."

Bella arranged the folder on her lap, sifting through dozens of clipped articles. "All of these deaths happened in Sziveria?"

"Yes, but not all of the singers are from here." Henley sat forward and wiggled her index finger. "If you check in the back there, I've compiled a list."

Markus reached over, his fingers brushing the inside of Bella's wrist on the way to the paper. A spark of awareness flitted across her skin, and she licked her lips. Somehow, she managed not to look at him. He looked over the efficient table of information. Over a dozen names, ages, and ethnicities filled the page. Linettie was the last entry.

"I've gathered as many articles relating to the women that I could find, both professional and concerning their deaths." Henley took a deep breath. "The seventh name on the list is my sister, Patricia Marcos. We have... had... different fathers."

"Why would you harass Linettie?" Markus asked.

Henley rolled her eyes. "I wasn't harassing her. I was trying to warn her." She tucked hair behind her ear in a nervous gesture. "A couple years ago, I tried to infiltrate Adelaine's home by applying to be a student. Normally, she wouldn't see me, I was too old, but I managed to beg a singer from Gaula to write a recommendation for me. I'd hoped I had enough of my sister's talent to at least tempt Adelaine to work with me, but I..."

Henley's face flushed and she shook her head, humming in embarrassment. "I sang two notes and she thanked me for my interest and sent me on my way. Once I realized I couldn't get information that way, I had to try something else. None of the others believed me either, and Adelaine started warning her students against me, that I was a crazed jealous want-to-be singer."

Markus held up the paper. "You think, what? That Adelaine Waynick is somehow killing these women?"

Grim determination hardened her face, exposing fine lines of age. "I don't think, I know."

Bella sifted through the articles on her lap again. At the beautiful faces of the women drawn for the editorials about their lives, cut abruptly short. She picked up the one about Patricia Marcos, found dead in her hotel suite in Port Ice Hollows, after arriving from Westica on a late-night ship. "It says your sister died of an unknown food allergy? She had a severe allergic reaction and was unable to alert anyone to receive medical treatment."

"Her food allergy was known, but the item she was allergic to is very rare. So rare, unless she visited somewhere wealthy enough for the host to *possibly* be serving them, she didn't have to worry about it. Certainly not in a dock city. The hotel owner, who also cooked all the meals, says she never in life had even seen a peanut, let alone put one in my sister's food."

Bella frowned. "A pea-nut? What is that?"

"It's a ground legume," Markus answered. "Very rare, very expensive, grown mostly in southern Westica. There are a few small producers on Miami Island, and in New Columbia. It's New Columbia's most profitable export and they're looking to expand to Westica's production level."

"Patricia discovered her allergy while in New Columbia on her first tour. The allergy was known in the county and handled in time." Henley looked out the window, her gaze moving. "I imagine for a while she was very nervous about what was served at the wealthier homes she visited and made it a point to ask about peanuts."

"How would Adelaine have found out?" Bella asked. "From our short time with her, she was adamant she didn't allow personal conversation to monopolize her time."

"I don't know about that," Henley said. "We didn't talk much about Adelaine when I was able to see Patricia. I just know peanuts here in Sziveria are so rare, to be killed by the allergy, it had to be someone close to her, someone she knew."

"Nothing with peanuts as the ingredient, such as chocolates or crackers that she may have brought for a friend, were found in her room?" Markus asked.

Henley shook her head. "No. They figured it somehow came from the kitchen at the hotel, despite what the owner said. That maybe another guest came downstairs and prepared something on the same counter with peanuts that the owner then cooked on, transferring pieces to Patricia's food without anyone knowing."

The deduction seemed likely to Bella, too.

The grieving woman, despite her sister being gone for many years, was still looking for a reason her sister died. Something other than bad luck.

Henley seemed to realize their doubt in her claims. She perched on the end of her chair, hands pressed together in pleading. "Please believe me. Don't let another singer die. Maybe Patricia's death *was* an accident, her being a student of Adelaine Waynick a coincidence. But the others? Please look at them all before you decide."

"We will," Markus assured, placing the list carefully back in the folder.

Bella arranged the clippings to keep them from falling out. "Are you okay with us taking this?"

"Please do. And thank you." Henley walked them to the door. She touched Markus's sleeve and Bella resisted the urge to bat the woman's hand free. "Please keep me informed."

Markus nodded, taking two steps down, out of her reach. Lunah slid between them, her tail swishing along Henley's pants, leaving behind dog hair. Henley gasped in dismay and stepped back through the threshold. Bella snorted internally. *That's right lady, he comes with the wolf.* Bella scratched Lunah's ear, smiling. The wolf licked her wrist and puffed warm air from her moist nose against Bella's skin.

Markus placed his hand on Bella's back and guided her to the sidewalk. Lunah trailed behind them. He hailed a carriage and instructed the driver to take them to the archives building. Bella raised her brows when he jumped inside after her.

"Archives?" she asked.

"I want to see if there's more information on these other singers than what Miss Jasper has collected," he answered.

"You believe her?"

He shrugged, moving Lunah's tail out of the way before closing them inside. "I don't know. Maybe. You have to admit, that's a lot of dead singers over a relatively short amount of time. And they were all young."

Bella brushed her fingers along the files edge in thought. "I'll look for articles about the Monaco Sands venues."

Without having to ask, he lifted his hand and she handed him Henley's research. The carriage rocked over brick. The faint crinkle of pages being flipped joined the muted rumble of wooden wheels. In a slow kaleidoscope of colored brick buildings, stone, and people, the city passed outside her window. Bella rubbed the toe of her shoe along Lunah's side. The wolf rolled, giving access to her belly, her tongue flopping out of her mouth on a happy groan.

"How is it," Markus asked slowly without looking up from where he arranged papers in the file open on his lap, "a woman in her twenties hasn't even been properly kissed? Is this country so afraid of intimacy?"

Bella stared at him in surprise. "No."

He lifted his eyes. "No?" When she didn't expound, he asked, "You are in your twenties, aren't you?"

"Twenty-three," she answered.

"You're beautiful, intelligent, and passionate. How has no other man discovered this?"

She flushed with equal parts pleasure and embarrassment. "Because all the other men would have cared about is the..." She waved a hand in annoyance. "The passion. And I doubt it would have been even that for them."

An expression she couldn't discern crossed over his face. His eyes darkened. "Did someone do something to you?"

No one wanted me, she somehow kept herself from saying. She cleared her throat and shook her head. "No."

"And you were never curious enough to?"

Covering her burning face with her hands, she squeezed her eyes shut and wondered how to explain. He'd told her quite a lot of personal details about his life yesterday. Details she hadn't asked for, and hadn't known she wanted until she learned them.

Despite knowing a future together couldn't happen, Markus fascinated her. For the first time in her life, a man made her consider throwing her rules to the wind and allowing herself, just once, to experience the physical between a man and woman. Then reality would interfere. She didn't want only *one* night. She wanted *years* of desire, of passion, of the ebb and flow in a relationship.

"I don't want anyone to have that memory of me," she finally said. "I don't want a man who doesn't want me in his life for longer than a lust-induced moment to know those things about me. I know that probably doesn't make much sense, but that's why." *And it drives me crazy that there are women in your country who have those memories of you,* she added in her mind, hoping she looked away before he saw the jealousy in her gaze.

"Hmm," he chimed, as if surprised. "That is a great deal of self-insight. I won't tell you what knowing this does to me. Not yet."

She blinked. "To you?"

"Oh *dak*," he growled in a low, sexy tone.

The alluring memory of his tongue sliding along hers, his fingers exploring a path, delivering sensations she hadn't known existed before, made her stomach flip. Bella's gaze locked with the molten heat in Markus's. A rumbling whine left Lunah. The wolf twisted on her back, trying to get Bella to return to her attention.

"Markus," Bella began on a sigh. She rubbed her toes along Lunah's ribs.

He held up a hand. "*Vye*. No. No excuses, no reasons why you aren't good enough for me, or why nothing between us could work. I don't care about any of that right now. I just... I want to know you. Is that okay?"

"Why?" she asked, her hands open in question. "Why is knowing me so important to you?"

SEVEN

Because you're my mate. He had to bite his tongue to keep from saying the words. Lunah flipped onto her paws and met his stare. The enticing confession she'd given continued to play havoc with him inside. He adjusted in his seat, thankful the pants he wore were lose, and his jacket was long, to cover the effect of her words. If he hadn't been tempted to claim her before, that would have been the tipping point.

She waited in silent expectation. He needed to answer.

Tell her, just tell her, Lunah urged, bumping her nose along his shin.

No. She isn't ready yet. Markus brushed his fingers along the fuzzy tips of her ears.

Perhaps a version of the truth, which would be startling enough for her, would be appropriate. "I don't think it's any big revelation to you that I want you. And I was curious how you could be so very inexperienced at an

age where most have at least been in one contract, if not one fling in their teenage years."

Her cheeks darkened pink. "Well, not me."

"*Dak*, I know that now."

"And?" she prompted, staring at him in
question.

"And what? I still want you. Very much."

The color increased in her face. "That's an
impossibility."

He arched a brow. "I disagree. I'm sure I
know what I want."

"You can't have me," she snapped and
looked away from him, nostrils flaring.

"You are," he whispered, knowing deep in
his heart the words she bit back. "You *are*
worth whatever you think I'd have to give up,
Bella."

She shook her head, the betraying sheen of
tears glistening in her ocean-colored
eyes. "No."

Markus almost told her. He opened his
mouth, the words forming in his throat.
There'd never be anyone else for him ever
again. But the carriage slowed. The heavy
shadow of the archives building darkened the
cabin. Bella was out the door before Markus
could help, Lunah leaping down after her.
Markus closed the file and unfolded himself
from the interior into the cool autumn day.
Heavy clouds filled the sky with the promise of
icy rain.

Hunched into her jacket, Bella waited for
him at the doorway, Lunah at her side. Wind

teased the loose curls around her face and pinkened her nose. Markus opened the door so she wouldn't have to remove her hands from the warmth of her pockets. He waited for both to enter before sliding in behind. Remembering the process from his previous investigation in the spring, Markus approached the aging ladies seated at the information table. He handed over a list of all the articles he needed. Bella spoke of what she was wanting, unsure exactly what would be best. The archivist told her travel articles, and any donated brochures would help her find what she wanted to know. They disappeared into the depths of endless shelves. Markus followed his host in a different direction. Lunah whined, but followed him.

Almost an hour later, arms burdened with files, Markus found Bella at a table in front of a wide window. There were no lamps at the archives. A ceiling of glass and large windows provided light. The building was closed from an hour before sunset to an hour after sunrise. Glancing up at the sky, he noted they didn't have too much time.

"Find what you needed?" he asked, setting the files across the table from her.

"I think so. Five years ago, The Blue Space was the most prestigious venue a musician, dancer, or artistic group could hope to be invited to play in," she said. "I can't find anything negative to explain why that might have changed."

"Linettie was booked to sing there when

she returned to Monaco Sands, wasn't she?" Markus pulled out the chair and sat. He opened the top folder, noting where on the list of deceased singers the name of the woman he researched was located. He put a small check.

"Yes, but Adelaine recommended somewhere different." Bella held up a flyer. "Ivory Notes Hall of Sound." She turned it toward herself and read, "Superior performances at discounted prices. Don't miss your next great show. Entertainment guaranteed."

Markus rubbed his chin, whiskers scratching against his knuckles. "Huh. She must have figured you wouldn't research that."

"And her recommending something would make it look like she was trying to help her former student." Bella fanned the pamphlet across her face. "Okay. So why would she do that?"

Markus shrugged. "I don't know much about the music industry. Maybe she'd sell more tickets at a discount venue."

"Or maybe..." Bella sighed and shook her head.

"Or maybe Adelaine was jealous of her student," Markus said, finishing the thought Bella didn't seem to want to.

Bella's face scrunched into a grimace. "Do you really think that? I mean, don't masters pride themselves on the success of their apprentices?"

Without looking up from the folder he

flipped through, he answered, "I guess that depends on the master."

She fell silent then. Markus allowed himself to be sucked into the investigation until the dying light and the sound of the closing bell pulled him from the information. Sighing, he sat back and slid his fingers into his hair.

"I'm going to have to talk to these other families." Cursing in frustration, he flipped a folder closed. "I was really hoping she was mistaken."

"You think there's a connection?" Bella asked, her beautiful eyes luminous in the golden light of evening.

"Yes." With another heavy exhale, he dropped the file on the haphazard stack. "Four of articles on the victims listed Adelaine Waynick's association with the girls. I need to speak with the families of the others to find out if she taught them."

"And check the passenger manifests at Import and Immigration," Bella reminded him, pushing at the corner of a brochure nearest to her. "Unless you think that's a dead end now."

"No, I'll check. If someone is targeting these singers, it'd make sense Adelaine is a common connection since she does train them. If one of the men show up on the passenger list, maybe he'll be known in the industry, and I can ask her if she knew of his possible involvement with her other students."

"Except they never discussed personal matters."

Markus shook his head. "That won't matter. She'd still have heard rumors of a predator patron amongst the community."

Bella picked up the list. "Someone older then, since some of these cases happened almost thirty years ago."

The closing bell chimed again. Lunah's ears twitched as she looked in the direction of the offending noise. Markus stood and organized all his notes into the folder. He handed it off to Bella and waited for her to slip Henley's file into her bag before placing the strap across her chest.

"Did you learn anything else interesting?" he asked as they navigated the maze of shelving units.

"No, only confirmed my initial discovery that the venue The Blue Space is what every artist hopes to be invited to perform in. I don't know why Adelaine told us she recommended Linettie play elsewhere."

"Like I said, she probably wanted to sound like she was being useful."

"Then why not tell us she recommended Linettie play there? We'd assume Adelaine helped her procure the spot."

Markus considered the angles. "Maybe she wanted us to doubt Linettie's talent in the end, that she was only good enough to play on bargain stages."

Bella shook her head. "Linettie would have known anywhere else would be a step down. She probably bragged the invitation, and acceptance, to Adelaine during her visit. And maybe Adelaine did recommend the discount venue because of jealousy, trying to convince herself Linettie was only worth performing there."

Markus mirrored her frown. "And Linettie ended up dead hours later."

THE TRIP to Import and Immigration had yielded no results. Bella could practically sense the frustration vibrating off Markus on the carriage ride to The Rows. His knuckles rasped along his bearded jaw, his focus intent on the darkening city passing by.

"Do you think you'd be able to check any information on the women at the SNID? If there are any case files on them?" he asked.

"I could, yes. I can also go to the records department, if you'd like."

Markus nodded, still watching beyond the window. "That might be a good idea. Just confirm cause of death. Not all the articles listed what happened to these women. I'm going to talk to the families that did mention the causes and match what Henley had written down, so I have at least a confirmed fact at the start of the interview."

"Do you think all the families will talk to you?"

"Maybe if they know there's an open investigation, even if it's private, and they want answers too, they'll be eager to tell me their story."

When he fell into silence again, the whisper of his beard being stroked joining the muted rumble of the road beneath them, Bella reached down and stroked Lunah's ears. The wolf turned and laid her head on Bella's thighs. She smoothed the darker fur along her muzzle and followed the lighter shade under her eyes and around to her dark ears.

"Such a pretty girl," she whispered, starting the process over again.

Lunah chuffed softly, her muzzle billowing. Bella chuckled, flapping the wolf's fuzzy ears between her fingers. With a playful whine, Lunah twisted her head on Bella's lap, her sharp teeth giving her a macabre upside-down grin. Laughing, Bella snatched her hand away while Lunah attempted to grab her fingers. She teased the silly wolf by rubbing under her chin, along her nose, and over her jaw whenever the dog missed her chance, likely on purpose, since Bella wasn't faster. Which only made Bella laugh louder, happiness spreading through her. She glanced up to find Markus watching her, an odd expression on his face.

"What?" she asked, returning her attention to Lunah, now nipping gently at the tips of her fingers.

"Nothing," he said, his voice rough.

Looking back at him, she drew her brows together. "Nothing?"

"She just..." he motioned at Lunah, "she never acts like this with anyone but me."

Bella chuckled, flicking her fingertips against the sharp points of Lunah's canines while the dog made vicious growling sounds. "Jealous?"

"*Vye*," he whispered, shaking his head. He returned to looking out the window. "Not jealous at all."

Confused, Bella stared at him, her fingers still near Lunah's mouth. The wolf carefully explored, using her tongue and teeth to map Bella's hand. Warm, sticky drool coated her palm, distracting her from Markus's strange behavior. The carriage slowed and rattled to a stop. Scrunching her nose, Bella wiped her damp hand on her pants. Lunah's ears perked forward a second before she faced the door.

Light and cold air flooded the interior without warning. Lunah leapt up, snarling and snapping between deep, threatening barks. A startled shout, and something metal hitting the ground, sounded before the door flapped and banged against the outside of the carriage.

Markus jumped through the opening, shouting a command Bella didn't understand. Lunah sat, silent. Her large form blocked the exit. Bella clutched her bag to her chest, straining to hear anything beyond the small cage the carriage had suddenly become.

"Did you have anything to do with this?" Markus's growled question filtered in.

"N-no! I'm an independent driver." Desperation clung to every word the carriageman uttered. "I can't afford to have a bad reputation. I swear, I had no idea they'd be waiting."

Bella shifted closer to the opening. Lunah glanced at her, nipping at the air in warning before returning her attention to the doorway. Now, Bella had to decide if she wanted to test the wolf or wait for the obvious permission from the beast master. Bella slid her fingers in a gentle caress through the thick fur between Lunah's shoulders. The wolf spoke, a low beseeching whine.

"Stay inside, Bella," Markus ordered.

"Tattler," Bella grumbled at Lunah, removing her hand. Lunah looked over her shoulder again, talking in her unique way.

"She says she'd like you to keep touching her," Markus said, still beyond her line of sight.

"Well, she should have thought about that before she decided to snitch."

Markus appeared in the frame. His hands gripped the top of the carriage, a hulking shadow against the blinding ball of the setting sun at his back. "She was obeying a command," he said softly. "Her only priority was keeping you safe, inside."

"What happened?" she asked. "And can I come out *now*?"

He stepped to side and gave a sharp gesture. Lunah jumped free in a graceful arc. The wind teased the black tips of her silver fur. Bella followed, unable to ignore the flash of a blade twirling in Markus's hand. The movement was hypnotic. Elegant and constant, made more mesmerizing by the little glints from the rings he wore.

"It's not even dark yet, and someone thought to rob this carriage," Markus said. The flash of the blade stopped and then disappeared altogether behind his back in a gesture she would have missed if she hadn't been watching.

Bella blinked. "Impressive."

"This doesn't surprise you?"

The carriage creaked in a jolt of motion, ambling away from them to fade into the slow progress of traffic down the avenue. Bella sighed and started their journey into the narrow streets of The Rows.

"No, not really," she answered.

Markus fell instep beside her, Lunah trailing behind. "Does this happen often?"

"It happens. Never to me before, no. But hired carriages are always at risk of being robbed since the riders have the money to pay for the fare."

Long shadows stretched along the road. Markus seemed to search each narrow space between the ramshackle houses. "And walking home?"

"Aside from being taunted by the occasional sex-hustler, no one really bothers anyone else. No one wants the attention," Bella said.

Markus shook his head. "I don't like it."

"You don't have to," Bella said, unable to stop the rise of her chin.

He stepped in close, taking her hand in his. The rasp of his dry palm, so much larger than hers, slid along her skin. "Is it such a terrible thing, my wanting something better for you?"

Tingles danced up her arm. His scent made the awareness so much *more*. "You shouldn't feel any responsibility for my circumstances."

"And yet I do." His hip bumped hers before she could speak. "If I were in a troubling situation, wouldn't you wish to help?"

"But I'm not in trouble," she argued.

He paused, forcing her to stop as well. He looked around, and she followed his gaze, taking in the pot-holed narrow street, the broken brick sidewalk, and sagging porches. Over the years, anytime the city attempted to replace missing or broken brick, the residents would steal the new blocks in the night. As a result, road maintenance in The Rows became almost nonexistent. Bella figured at this point, returning the roads to dirt might be better in some ways.

His golden eyes, molten in the rays shining between the houses, caught hers. "Aren't you?"

Concern shone in his gaze and Bella swore she could *feel* his stress, his fear over her circumstances. But that was impossible. Wasn't it? She wanted to touch his face, soothe his worries. She fisted her hand and tugged on his hand to get him walking again. "We've lived here for three years now, and we've been okay."

"I would prefer better than okay for you. You deserve more."

"As does everyone else stuck here," she said, sweeping her arm to include everything they walked past. "We have a roof over our head and food on our table every night. I have clothes to wear that aren't stained and thread-bare, and enough wood to keep us warm through the night. What more do I need?"

Markus clamped his mouth shut on the words he wanted to say. Words that wouldn't matter to her, or even make much sense. Instead, he shrugged and watched more closely than usual the darkened areas they passed. Despite having lost their weapon, the two would-be thieves were still out there, waiting to pounce on a victim. He fell a little behind, following her deeper into the dilapidated neighborhood.

An aging man beat dust from a rug on his sagging porch. Sun caught the fine particles billowing in a golden cloud around him. Two dogs fought in a front yard over a discarded bag of street food. A cat hissed and danced sideways when they passed too close to the broken hollowed out stairs where she'd likely stashed her kittens.

Markus couldn't help but compare the weight of desperation around him to the quiet freedom surrounding his home in Ruthenia. A modest cabin far enough away from civilization to allow Lunah to wander, but close enough to wade through feet of snow in the depths of winter if he needed something from town. Ruthenian culture had kept cities from becoming cramped spaces of decay. Communities were small, tight knit, usually no greater than a few hundred. Port cities were the exception, but micro communities blossomed within the city streets.

Families linked together through marriage kept bonds tight. Preserved the fragile layers of society. Markus had no idea if family bonds remained after marriage in Sziveria. Since he had yet to meet either of Bella's siblings, and so many people seemed left to fend for themselves without any assistance from the communities around them, he had to figure probably not.

"Why did your brother and sister choose not to help you?" Markus asked.

She shoved her hands into her pockets, hunching her shoulders. They turned the corner. A bicyclist sped by, the faint whir of chain and spokes joining the argument of two neighbors, hanging out their side windows hurling insults. Smoke from woodstove pipes and chimneys hazed the cooling evening air.

Bella heaved an exaggerated sigh, squinting against the bright sun streaking across the sidewalk. "I think anger, at first. They were too upset with what my father had done, it was easier to ignore the situation my mother had been put in rather than face her sudden fall into poverty at his hands."

"Why leave her alone? Why didn't you both move in with one of them?" he asked, still struggling to understand the dynamics.

"I don't know. I haven't spoken to either of them since Papa died," she admitted, her unhappiness evident in her clenched jaw and flared nostrils.

"Talking about this upsets you."

"Of course, it upsets me," she snapped and then sighed. "Sorry, but I mean come on. She's *our mother*. Why was it me, the youngest, who didn't even have a job when our father died, end up becoming the most responsible? And, fine," she continued, her words tumbling from her mouth faster, "I get it, they have kids and were scared of Hossman. He has a terrible reputation. But I know for a fact Junie could have helped us, but she refused to even ask her husband. Lemar, the pride of my father, didn't even bother to help us move, because oh, the horror if someone recognized him in The Rows."

"What does he do that his reputation is so much more important than his family?" Markus asked.

Bella scoffed and shook her head, disgust twisting her features. Looking away, she licked her lips. "His family. His wife is the daughter of an Extilis Square store owner. Lemar is his assistant. He feared if his father-in-law found out how irresponsible our father had been at the end of his life, getting involved with Hossman and his lending schemes, he'd not only lose his position, but his wife."

"I didn't think that was possible."

"It's not legally, but Lemar's father-in-law could send him on an inventory expedition to anywhere in the world that my brother would never return from." Her shoulders rolled. "I don't know the man to know if that's Lemar's fear, or if he's just embarrassed by our situation."

She needs calmed, she needs, Lunah urged, her nose bumping into the back of Markus's thigh.

Markus pulled Bella's hand free from her pocket and laced their fingers together. Tiny tendrils of awareness sparked across his skin. He wanted to explore the texture of her palm, her forearm. Find out if the teasing caress would excite her. The simple, yet sensual exploration would have to wait. "The circumstances are not your fault. Your brother and sister are fools for being willing to lose you."

"I don't know," she said, her words laced with frustration. "I mean if you were to marry outside of Ruthenia, would your siblings support your choice and visit you? Would they welcome your spouse into their home? Your children?"

Markus recoiled. His fingers tightened around her hand. "How is that the same? Neither you nor your mother made the decision to lose everything, to have to live," he waved his free hand around, "here. If I were to choose outside of our social norms, to forsake tradition and remove *myself* from my family, that would be different."

"But would they support you?" she asked, stopping and forcing him to do the same. She tugged on his hand until he turned to face her. "Would they understand?"

Markus searched her beautiful eyes, vivid in the shaft of light spilling between two houses. She was so gorgeous to him. He touched a finger to her jaw, tracing the delicate line to her ear. "I don't know."

"For Lemar and Junie, our fall into The Rows, into extreme poverty, owing so much we can't afford to live in anything better, was a social disgrace. One neither of them could accept. So, they didn't. I may never forgive them for it. I want to, I know I need to, but right now, I can't. My mother loves her children, and her grandchildren, and refuses to allow the rift to cost more than it already has. She does what they refuse. She visits. She remembers them every Wintervail and provides gifts for their Wintervail chest we can't afford. She never forgets a birthday."

"While they forget about her, and you." He rubbed his thumb along the back of her hand.

"I know it's their decision, but it still hurts." She tugged her hand free and shoved it back into her pocket, away from him and began walking again. "Think really hard before you force your family to make a similar choice."

"If they can't accept how I choose to live my life, then perhaps they don't deserve to be part of it." Markus chose to ignore her closed body language, sliding his arm around her shoulders and pulling her into his side. "Your siblings are the ones missing out. They will never know what an amazing sister they have in you."

"I'm sure they feel the same way about themselves," she stated in a dry tone. "They're so amazing they won't set foot in my home."

Laughing, Markus squeezed her shoulder. "Oh, do I hope I'm there when they finally, and they will, grace your door."

She snorted. "Why? It's going to be embarrassing, for everyone. Drama. Lots of drama."

He grinned. "It's going to be spectacular."

CHAPTER
EIGHT

Bella missed Markus. The lack of his presence created a physical ache in her chest. A heavy sensation she attempted to rub free without success. Where was he? Last night, before he'd left, they'd agreed to meet tonight at her house again, after he spoke to the families he could reach out to about the dead singers. She managed to get copies of a few public records pertaining to his case and she was anxious for his impression.

Well, and to see him. Bella wanted that with a desperation bordering on pathetic. Sighing, she dropped her head to the table on her folded arms.

"What is it, child?" Madeleine asked, her cool fingers brushing hair from Bella's temple. "Tough case?"

"Markus was supposed to be here before dinner."

"Perhaps Wolvenguard needed help with

something. Two wolves are surely better than one, and safer," her mother suggested.

Another tight fist lodged in Bella's chest. Groaning, she buried her face deeper against her arms. "I just thought he'd, I don't know, send me a note?"

"Maybe there wasn't time."

Spreading her arms across the table she sat up. "Yeah, maybe."

Madeleine wrapped Bella in a hug from behind. "Nothing has changed. He hasn't left the country without a word, never to be seen again. He cares about you, I promise."

Until now, Bella hadn't wanted to know her mother's perception of Markus. Madeleine had a unique gift of recognizing the compatibility between two people. She used her talent to help solidify matches and to counsel. Bella knew, if they could ever manage to pay off her father's debt, her mother's dream was to become a fulltime matchmaker. The insecure part of Bella rose like a dark shadow. Deep inside, she knew how Markus felt about her. At least, she figured she knew. He cared, more than he should, more than she wanted him to, but with his absence she needed the assurance.

"Have you felt anything from him?" Bella asked, wrapping her fingers around her mother's forearm still draped across her upper chest.

"Oh, yes. You never want to know about the men who may suite you, though. What has changed?"

Bella's heart flipped. "He suites me?"

Madeleine kissed Bella's temple before straightening. "Daughter, he was made for you. Or rather, I suppose, you were made for him, since it is *you* who control the fate of your relationship with him."

Bella turned in the chair, grabbing the backrest. "I don't understand."

Madeleine cupped her jaw. Her gaze held compassion and a hint of an alarming sadness. What did her mother know that Bella didn't?

"Markus is a beast master," Madeleine stated as if Bella should know what the declaration meant.

"Yes, I'm aware. Lunah makes it hard to forget."

Sighing, Madeleine grabbed the nearest chair and pulled it close to sit facing Bella. "No, you don't understand. Beast master's bond with their mates. It's forever, Bella, contract or no. He can't ever bond with anyone else, even if you were to reject him."

"That doesn't seem fair."

"No, perhaps not, but it's the way of things, how Ruthenian's are genetically created."

"But I'm Sziverian," she protested.

Madeleine grasped Bella's hand between both of hers and squeezed. "With just enough Ruthenian from a past ancestor, probably on your father's side, to have a genetically inherited talent. Bella, what you can do..." Her mother shook her head. "It's nothing short of incredible."

More arguments rose within Bella. "Ruthenia would never accept me, so how could Markus?"

Madeleine stroked the back of Bella's hand in a soothing motion. "Child, he won't have a choice."

Confused, Bella pulled her hand free and stared at her mother. "What do you mean he won't have a choice?"

Rising, Madeleine turned away. "I don't know enough for the rest of this conversation. You'll need to have a long talk with Markus, when he's ready."

"When he's ready? Mother, there's no conversation to have. I'm not going to ask him to marry into genetics his country would never recognize, let alone give up said country."

Over her shoulder, Madeleine met Bella's gaze. "Don't you think that's up to Markus?"

Right. Up to Markus, who'd disappeared on her. Anxiety and concern gnawed at Bella's insides. Time inched closer to the arctic winds closing travel, but they hadn't blown down far enough yet. Markus wasn't one for games, either. If he'd changed his mind about wanting her help, he'd have said as much. Something was wrong. Bella knew on a visceral level she didn't understand, something bad had happened to Markus.

Pressing her palms to the table in determination, she rose. "I have to go to Wolvenguard's."

Madeleine glanced at the back windows

and shook her head. "Not in the dark you aren't. You know it's not safe, Bella."

"But—"

"No." Madeleine grabbed a wet washcloth and wiped down the meager counter space in the kitchenette. "You can go in the morning, at first light if you can make yourself get up that early, but not tonight. If something has happened, it won't do him any good to have you robbed or worse."

The daring attempt to rob their carriage yesterday, before the sun had even set, made Bella hesitate. Her mother was right, she couldn't go anywhere tonight. Sighing in frustration, she gathered all the documents she'd set aside. "I wish we had a radio."

"If we could afford a personal radio, we wouldn't be living in The Rows."

"He's in trouble, I know it," Bella whispered.

Madeleine stilled. "First thing in the morning, understand?"

Bella nodded. "First light."

REALITY SHIFTED for Markus in an odd slide of semi-consciousness, haze, warbled voices and jostled nerves. Rough hands yanked him, while booted feet shoved at his thighs. He fell from... he wasn't sure. A cart? A carriage? At some point, he thought he felt and heard brick switch to gravel under his head. Unable to support his weight on his arms, let alone his legs, the ground met him in a harsh impact. Rocks dug into the exposed skin at his hip and bit into his elbow and cheek.

"How am I supposed to get him inside?" an angry male voice whined. "He weighs twice what I do."

"And three times what I do," a woman answered. "We'll each take an arm and drag him inside."

Helpless, Markus could do nothing, not even speak, when the man and woman wrenched on his arms. Fingernails dug into the sensitive flesh of the underside of his biceps. They dragged him in long, heaving pulls, along gravel that transitioned to stairs, his legs and tailbone bumping each rise in painful jostles. At the top of wherever they'd taken him, they dropped him. His shoulders and head bounced on wooden planks. The clank of lock and key, followed by hinges creaking told him he probably laid on a porch.

In the distance a crow cawed. The faint buzz of insects and lack of road sounds meant they'd likely taken him beyond the city. Markus tried, and failed, to open his eyes. No part of his body obeyed him. The same fiery sensation he'd experienced between bouts of awareness sheered across his nerve endings. When the darkness crept in again, he welcomed the oblivion.

Muted, as though coming to him through a tube, Markus became slowly aware of the voices again.

"Let...give... more," a masculine voice warbled in and out. "I... we gave him enough... dead yet."

"No, the serum... expensive. He's dying, I... won't be long... lock... door... tranquilizer... kill him... elements will. No... find him here." The fragmented conversation made little sense. The woman was adamant, certain of whatever she told the man with her.

"... sure your information... correct? That... sedative is poisonous... him?"

"Yes," the woman snapped, her voice coming into sharp focus. "Drop him in the corner."

Pain scorched across Markus's muscles. He didn't even notice when he'd been released, only the relative relief of cold stone under his cheek, soothing the agony along his jaw.

"The drug broker won't cut you a deal for more sedative if we use the full amount of this second doses?" the man asked.

"I don't want to risk dealing with the broker again. I like the option of the anesthetic for another use."

The man sighed. "I know, I heard her yesterday during private lessons. She's—"

"Too good," the woman snarled. "She can't be allowed to even perform, do you understand? This winter, while the weather is too cold for anyone to even look for her, she'll be found after the spring thaw. Poor thing, wandered out in the cold and froze to death. So sad. Happens every year."

Hinges creaked again. "What about the woman he came to the house with?"

The door muffled their conversation, but not enough for him not to catch her answer. "She's a nobody. I asked a few discreet questions. She's a file clerk for the SNID and is of no concern. Besides, if both of them go missing, someone might investigate. You bought the ticket in his name on a ship for Ruthenia, correct?"

"Yes, before we grabbed him. Here." Paper rustled. "The purchase receipt and boarding pass."

Skin slapped skin. "Get that away from me! Destroy them at once, you fool! Do you *want* to be caught?"

The door opened and then slammed closed again. A key scraped in a lock. "Sorry, I thought you'd want to at least see them."

"I trust you, Flynn. You know that, don't you?" the woman crooned, her words clear even through the barrier. They hadn't moved from beyond the room they'd trapped him in. The door shook in the frame as if a weight had fallen onto it. "You know how important you are to me. How much it means to have you at my side. In all things."

Realization dawned in Markus's foggy brain. Flynn Evers. Which meant the woman was...

"Adelaine," Flynn's voice groaned through the door. "Shouldn't we... Oh summer sun," he breathed on a groan.

"I want to celebrate our victory, right now." A buckle jangled and leather slithered through fabric. "Don't make me wait."

"I can never make you wait, for anything," he said, his words holding an edge of anger along with resignation.

Markus tried to lick his lips, move his fingers, his toes, *anything*. But everything remained frozen. Frustrated, he focused on his breathing. Beyond the door, the muffled moans and grunting of sex interrupted his already lacking concentration. The passionless coupling was over within minutes. Small favors.

"Do you have everything? We left nothing behind?" Adelaine asked, her words breathy.

"Just the man," Flynn chuckled.

"I meant your clothes. It's going to be a cold ride home. I don't need you freezing on me."

Their voices faded. Markus tried again to move, this time able to lift himself enough to keep from choking on vomit when his stomach protested whatever toxin they'd managed to inject in him. Memory was a fuzzy, useless thing to him. He couldn't remember how they'd managed to sneak up on him, let alone get close enough to give him something strong enough to render him inept.

Markus rolled away from the nasty puddle he'd made, thankful for the ability to move even a few inches. Thread by invisible thread, he sought his bond. *Lunah...*

Markus, my Markus! Her anxious voice exploded through his mind. The scent of humid air and sounds of rustling leaves and barking assailed him.

He grimaced. He didn't have the energy to close any of the bonds now that he'd opened them. Markus waited until the throbbing pain subsided enough to take a more normal breath.

Where are you, my Markus, where are you? Lunah asked. Her desperate barks filtered along their link.

I don't know. I'm not... well. Markus swallowed against another bout of nausea. *I need you to find me, Lunah. Straes'ya vae'ny.*

"PLEASE," Bella begged, almost clutching her hands together and falling to her knees in pleading. "Please let me see Wolvenguard. He knows me, and I wouldn't ask if this weren't important."

"I already told you," the doorman replied, his face a stony mask, "he isn't home."

The sense of dread Bella had experienced last evening had intensified throughout the night until, restless and edgy, she'd leapt from bed and dressed. Darkness or not, she *needed* to see Markus. The compulsion couldn't be ignored. The gray of early morning barely brightened the sky when she'd arrived on Wolvenguard's doorstep. Deep in the house, a dog barked in frantic yelps. Bella's anxiety ratcheted up a notch.

"Do you know when he'll return?" she asked.

"I can't reveal that information."

"Can I at least take Lunah?" She tried to see over the guard's broad shoulder.

He leaned enough to block her view. "The wolf is in Wolvenguard's care and cannot leave the property."

Bella knew if she were to call to the wolf, Lunah would figure out a way to make it to her. Since Bella needed to be on Wolvenguard's good side, she didn't think he'd appreciate her destroying property, so she clenched her jaw and took a step back. "Can you please tell—"

The door closed before she could finish. She blew out a frustrated breath. "...Nick that I asked to see him. Thanks," she said to the wood panel. "Great, now what?"

Markus could be with Nick, though why he'd assist the arch guardian and leave Lunah behind, Bella didn't know. What she knew about beast masters could fit in the palm of her hand, with room to spare. She sat on the top front porch step and dropped her elbows onto her knees in thought. Aside from breaking into the greenhouse and absconding with Lunah, there wasn't anything else she could do but go home and later tonight hope Nick returned, or maybe Markus finally showed.

Rising, Bella brushed dirt off her pants. Heading down the street, she jerked the edges of her jacket closer together and tried not to feel so out of her depth walking among the grand houses of the Arch District. Wolven-guard's home was the only one not behind a gate. Two snarling wolves at the street warned visitors of the resident's beastly nature. Bella figured the knowledge of the massive wolf behind the door probably did the rest, no further security was necessary.

A low dawn fog rose in whisps from the brick street, making everything hazy shadows in the distance. Frost coated the wrought-iron bars of the fences and sparkled off leaves in the rising sun. Bella's breath left her in vapor puffs. Her nose ran from the chill and she sniffled, burying her hands into her pockets. At the corner, she hailed a hired carriage, climbing in without assistance.

She asked to be taken to The Rows after rejecting the thought to go to SNID and plead for help from Reyes Avner. If he wouldn't bother to help her keep her position as his assistant, he certainly wouldn't help her find a missing beast master. Especially a missing beast master that had shown the shield guardian over the division he had better investigation skills than the guardians under his authority. If Nick didn't show up by dinner, Bella would knock on his door again.

Halfway to her house, with the city waking up around her, an eerie, mournful howl split the air. A hush descended on the street. Even the birds fell silent. Bella turned, shading her eyes against the glare of the rising sun, and searched the misty road. Heart in her throat, she took a tentative step in the direction of the call.

"Please, please, please," she found herself whispering under her breath without thought.

A silver beast materialized from the rolling haze. Behind the wolf, a hulking shadow fought to keep up. Bella held a hand out to Lunah, her heart pounding in her ears. Hopeful tears burned her eyes. Lunah pranced, attempting to wrap herself around Bella while her tail danced in happy swooshes. Whines of joy joined her wiggling body. Bella sank her fingers into the thick pelt between Lunah's shoulders, holding tight as Nick, not Markus, stepped through the fog into sight. A dark brown wolf with cinnamon eyes stood at his hip.

Like Markus, Nick kept his ash blond hair braided in an intricate plait behind his back. The similarities stopped there, however. Nick was clean shaven, lanky to Markus's bulk, and closer to Bella in height. His skin was also closer to what Bella imagined from the sun-starved country, pale. She had learned skin tones were as varied in his country as in hers. Genetics still had a say. Her own pale brown to her mother's more golden, despite their own lack of yearly rays, was proof of that, a gift from her father's side of the family tree.

Nick shoved his hands into pockets of his long leather coat. The ends of a red, navy and gray striped scarf swayed halfway down his chest. "I'm so sorry. You should have been invited in and waiting to see me when I returned home only a few minutes after you left."

Bella swallowed against the dryness coating her mouth. "Where's Markus?"

Nick shrugged, his face twisting in helpless displeasure. "I don't know. He didn't come home last night, and I thought maybe he was with you. But he never would have left Lunah. I would have come to you first thing this morning, but there was a situation I had to handle. Lunah was a complete mess when I came home. She'd destroyed a wall and was working on a door when I released her. She bolted from the house and Iskov had to track her."

Thick puffs of vapor left Bella. She grasped Lunah's face between her cold fingers and met the dogs' brilliant golden eyes. "What's going on, Lunah girl?"

She gave a quiet woof. Bella sighed and shook her head.

"I don't know what to do," she said to the arch guardian.

"Let's get inside somewhere warm, preferably private, and I'll tell you."

Bella led them to her house. The warm, inviting scent of cinnamon filled the air. Madeleine was gone, but sticky buns and a cooling pot of tea sat on the table. Bella shrugged out of her jacket, hanging it on the back of the chair before sitting and picking up a gooey roll. She peeled off a layer, ate it, and offered the rest to Lunah.

"Okay, what's going on," she asked.

Nick sat, cautious, as though he worried about his welcome, or the strength of the spindle chair.

"It supports Markus, you won't break it," she said, exasperated.

He pointed at the rolls and Bella made a help-yourself motion. "Thanks," he said.

Bella stood, too anxious to be still, and went to wash the sugar from her fingers. "You know how to find Markus?"

"No."

Confused, Bella turned to stare at him while drying her hands. "But you said—"

"I can't," he pointed a piece of torn roll at Lunah, "but she can."

Bella's heart sank. "Neither of us can hear her."

Using his pinky, Nick scratched behind his ear. "Actually, that's not true."

"You can hear her?"

"Nope."

Bella resisted the urge to grab the salt-shaker and launch it at him. "Then what isn't true about our ability to communicate with her?" Bella asked, her words measured as her patience wore thin.

Nick stood and set the remaining piece of his roll on the plate. He joined her beside the sink, rinsing the sticky from his fingers. "There's folklore in Ruthenia that says, once upon a time, a mate to a beast master could also bond with their animal."

"Even if the mate wasn't a beast master?" Bella asked.

"Only if the mate didn't share the master's talent, actually." He accepted the towel from her and dried his hands. "See, a fellow beast master is already bonded to an animal and can't bond with their mates. But a non-beast talent doesn't have such restrictions, and the link shared with their mate allows them to also bond with the animal."

"And this no longer happens?"

Nick shrugged. "I don't know. Beast masters have only paired with other beast masters for generations. It's become an unbroken tradition in my homeland. The truth of the ability has been lost."

Lunah padded on quiet feet to Bella. Her warm, dry nose bumped Bella's hand. "And you think I can do this even though Markus and I aren't mated?"

Nick's cheeks puffed and he let out a long breath. "I think you may be bonded to him."

Bella stared at him. Denial punched her in the gut. "No."

"Yes."

She put distance between them, as much as her tiny living space would allow. "That's impossible," she argued, hands raised. "I can't be bonded to him. We haven't... I've only kissed him and from my understanding that isn't enough."

Nick glanced at Lunah and then back to Bella. He rubbed the back of his neck. "See, here's the thing, Lunah wouldn't come to you unless you were part of her pack. You'd only be part of her pack if you were her alpha's mate. Understand?"

Clenching her jaw, she absorbed the information. Lunah returned to her side, once again nudging her hand. "Would Markus have known?"

Nick tossed the towel on the counter. "I don't see how he wouldn't."

And he'd said nothing. Bella tried not to be wounded by the knowledge and failed. She'd been the one to advocate against their relationship growing beyond the small confines she'd delegated for them. Disappointment shouldn't have been an issue, and yet knowing he'd rejected her, rejected them, hurt all the same. Lunah whined, brushing Bella's fingers again.

"What happens if I bond with her? If I can somehow do that?"

Nick shoved his hands into his pockets. His attention shifted to his wolf, laying quiet in the small opening from the entrance hall to the living space. "I'm not sure. Probably make whatever bond you have with Markus permanent."

"Even if that's not what he wants?"

"The woman forms the bond, I can't imagine he'd say no, Bella."

Bella crossed her arms against the vulnerable choice placed before her. "If he knew and wanted..." She blew out a breath, forcing courage where none existed and tried again. "If he *knew*, and didn't say anything, don't you think that means he doesn't want to be stuck here, in Sziveria, with me?"

"I can't answer that."

She hugged herself tighter. The world compressed around her in a confusing jumble of fear, uncertainty, and the heartache of Markus's rejection.

When the silence stretched into long minutes, Nick asked, "What do you have to lose by trying?"

Markus. She had Markus to lose. Maybe he didn't want her, and maybe when she found him, she'd learn the awful truth. However, if he was never found, if he died out there wherever he was lost, he'd be gone forever. She'd never know. Would never get to see his smile or hear his words of encouragement. Or taste his kiss. The world, or at least hers, would be a darker, less-than place.

If Bella wanted him, she'd have to find him.

Sitting, she delved deep into her heart, her mind a vortex of what-ifs. Did *she* want Markus for her own? She glanced at Lunah. The wolf stared back, eyes pleading. Yes. Bella straightened her spine. Until he told her no, she'd lay claim to the beast master.

"Okay, tell me what to do," she said.

Nick shrugged out of his jacket and hung it over the back of the nearest chair. The scarf followed. "It may not be pleasant."

"I don't care."

He rolled up the sleeves of his dark green

sweater. "Do you have antiseptic and bandages?"

Bella's eyes widened. "Why would you need that?"

"I won't."

Bella pressed her palms to her temples. She refrained from growling in frustration. "Why will bandages be needed?"

"I don't know how much contact Lunah will need since you aren't a beast master or full blooded Ruthenian. She may just need skin to skin like a normal bonding, or she may need deeper." His gaze captured hers. "Much deeper."

Great. Bella's heart hammered to the point of pain. "In the bathroom, in a box under the sink."

He nodded. Iskov shifted out of the doorway but didn't bother to rise. Moments later, Nick returned, setting the small wooden crate on the table with a *thunk*. Digging around inside, he removed several objects, setting them on the table.

"Are you wearing anything under that tunic?" he asked, still sorting through the box.

"A tank," she answered, licking her dry lips.

"Take your shirt off, leave the tank."

Bella obeyed.

"On the floor, with Lunah."

Slowly, Bella lowered herself to the floor, her back to the couch.

Nick set a chair away from the table near her and sat. "You might want to lie down."

Bella slid her butt along the floor until she lay, her hair bunched in a tangle against the couch. Grit scraped her bare arms and the back of her neck. She resisted the urge to brush away the dirt caught in the rug.

"Repeat after me, as clearly as you can, Lunah *sza'vnica*. She will do the rest if she's able."

Lunah shook her head and whined. Iskov growled.

Nick spoke Ruthenian in a placating tone to them both. Iskov settled. Lunah laid her head on Bella's stomach.

A shiver of fear at the unknown raced through Bella. There would be no going back if the bond took place. No stopping any pain or undoing any permanent connection. She clamped her teeth together and waited until the tremble stopped in her limbs. Looking at the beautiful wolf, she whispered, "Lunah, *sza'vnica*."

Lunah touched her mouth to Bella's forearm. Bella's pulse thumped a rapid, uncomfortable beat in her ears. The wolf groaned in annoyance and opened her mouth, touching her tongue to Bella's skin. Anxiety quickened Bella's breathing until stars danced in front of her vision. She squeezed her eyes closed. Another sound of frustration left Lunah. Thick, sharp teeth pressed into Bella's forearm. Bella bit her tongue against a squeak of alarm, not wanting anything, including her unease, to stop the process.

Pressure built on Bella's forearm and pounded in her brain. The force increased in weight, dividing her focus between the agony in her forearm and the splitting in her mind. Like a knife twisting through her skull, a ribbon of pain pulsed through her head. The sharp ache of teeth piercing her skin made her scream. Nothing helped. Lunah didn't stop, and neither did the torment.

A golden thread, shimmery and gossamer, flared into life behind her closed eyes. The fine strand uncoiled and stretched tight, reverberating. On the other end, a strong female presence waited in anxious expectation.

Bella, my Bella! Lunah exclaimed, her voice ricocheting through Bella's mind.

Bella grabbed her head, shocked to find both her hands free. She curled into herself and tried to breathe through the hurt. Something warm dripped down her upper lip. Tears maybe. Sucking snot, a metallic taste at the back of her throat took her by surprise. She blinked open bleary eyes and looked straight into intense golden irises.

Please speak to me, please, Lunah whispered.

"I don't know how," Bella answered, blinking hot tears from her eyes.

That will work, that will, Lunah said, rising. She shook her entire frame and stepped over Bella to sit at her back.

Nick dropped into the space she'd been occupying. "Let me see your arm."

Bella rolled enough to raise her throbbing

left forearm. He handed her a square of gauze and tapped his nose. Blinking, Bella accepted the square and wiped under her nose. The gauze came away bloody.

"Did you hear her?" Nick asked, attending to her wound.

The pain in Bella's head masked his efforts. She hardly felt anything. "Y-yes, I can hear her. But..." She groaned and fisted the gauze in her hand. Pressing her fist to her forehead, she grimaced. Fresh tears burned behind her closed eyes. "Oh, it hurts."

"I'm not sure what to do about that or if it'll get better."

Bella figured right now her discomfort didn't matter. She turned her head and looked at Lunah. "Where is he, Lunah? Where's your alpha?"

CHAPTER

NINE

Markus spit acidic bile from his mouth. He'd long since run out of anything to expel, but his body still insisted on trying. Everything hurt. Nerve-endings burned, his muscles cramped, and a steady throb flowed in wave through his head. Somehow, he'd managed to drag himself away from the broken window and get himself into a sitting position. He didn't have anything else in him.

Chilled air whistled through the busted glass. Light glittered on the uneven edges. Dead leaves skittered along the stone floor. Markus figured at one time the room had been used for food storage. Old braces for shelves stuck out in random places along the walls.

He had no idea what time it was, or how long he'd been locked in the room. At some point after his kidnappers had dumped him, he'd passed out. How long he stayed under, he didn't know. The cold and need to empty his stomach had dragged him from unconsciousness. Off and on, he'd slipped back into the darkness, repeating the routine. Shivering and sick.

Through it all, his link to Lunah had remained a constant. He figured since his need to be in her presence had reached a desperate level, he'd been missing for at least a full day. Communication had dimmed to little more than sensation, a brief knowledge he wasn't alone. He no longer had the energy to speak with her. When she did attempt to communicate, her words were muffled, garbled, his headache too extreme to understand what she was trying to tell him. He kept the hope she'd find him. Somehow.

Markus dozed. The light faded from the room. The temperature dropped. Odd noises echoed beyond his prison. A dog yipped and barked, a high-pitched mixture of distressed excitement. Two voices blurred together. Markus lifted his drooping head toward the door. Claws scratched and the yipping turned frantic.

Lunah, Markus managed to force through their bond.

"Maybe you should wait," a male voice said. Markus blinked, his fuzzy brain recognizing the deep tenor. Nick Benirak. "Let me go in first."

"Why?" a woman asked, her sweet voice flowing over him like honey. Markus sagged in relief. Bella.

"Because, he might be—"

"He's not dead," she snapped. "Lunah said he's in there, she heard him. He's not dead. He's not."

Lunah said? Markus tried to untangle that statement, wondering if his addled brain had misunderstood.

"He might not want you to see him... the way he is," Nick said so softly Markus almost missed the words.

"I don't care. Not only am I going in, but I'm going in with the wolf, who will beat both of us in. Do something about this door. Now."

The door shuddered. Once, twice, splintering the doorframe on the third attempt. The fourth sent it flying open, bouncing off the wall with a loud bang. A cough turned into a gag. Markus could relate, he'd been dealing with the nasty he'd been forced to live in for however long he'd been locked in the small room. Lunah bounded in, settling over his outstretch legs, her muzzle under his chin, her paws on his chest. Her sharp nails bit through the fabric of his shirt, but he didn't care. He couldn't lift his hands to pet her.

Markus, my markus, she repeated over and over again, her tongue cleaning his neck and up to his hair.

Stop, I'm gross, he managed to convey through their link. He couldn't push her away and she didn't listen.

"Markus," Bella breathed, her voice weak

with tears. "Oh summer sun, what have they done to you?"

Markus could only grunt through his weakness.

"Damn you're a mess," Nick muttered. "Come on, let's get you home."

Nick hefted him up under his arms and slung him over his shoulder like a sack of potatoes. The action sent Markus's head spinning and he astonishingly didn't make a mess down the back of Nick's jacket.

Nick laid him in the back of a carriage, throwing a blanket over him. Lunah climbed in and settled on the seat above him. Bella sat on the floor with him, pillowing his head on her lap. She smoothed her fingers through his filthy, tangled hair.

"You're safe. You're going to be okay," she whispered as the carriage jostled into motion.

Markus let his guard drop and drifted into sweet oblivion.

BELLA HELPED Markus sip cold tea from a glass. Steam floated from the hot water he lay submerged in. After nearly an hour of slow, constant drinking and refreshing of hot water, he'd lost some of the gray pallor. The moment they arrived at Wolvenguard's, Nick had leapt from the driver's seat, sent help to get Markus to his room and had disappeared.

By the time he returned, Bella had Markus in the empty tub and was in the process of shoving aside her virginal discomfort to un-dress the very large, very sick, man. Nick had the Arch Guardian Eslainte in tow, a true Medpath Gen-Heir, which Bella found fasci-nating. With a touch of her fingers, Eslainte had diagnosed and went about treating Markus. The tea he now sipped cautiously was of her making, meant to hydrate while simultaneously helping his body expel the toxins. Certain sedatives, Eslainte had ex-plained, can be very dangerous to a Ruthenian.

Someone had tranquilized him and then left him to die. She'd cried, fat silent tears she refused to let him see while she'd washed his hair. Her heart had broken at the loss she'd al-most had to endure. The fear and anxiety forced her to recognize he'd come to mean more than she realized. Yes, she'd gone to ex-tremes to find him, doing what she thought of as impossible. He was a vital man, who be-lieved in her in a way no one else ever had, and she couldn't sit around and let him stay lost. Her reasons at the time seemed clear. Only, with her hands in his hair, the warmth of his bare skin under her fingertips, she knew she'd been lying to herself.

She loved him.

Love had motivated her actions, even if she didn't admit it at the time. And somehow, she was going to have to tell him she'd taken away his choice in a mate. Either he accepted her, or, if Nick was to be believed, he lived his life alone. Bella didn't want to do that to him. He deserved so much more.

Taking a deep breath, she lowered the glass and reached to help him sit up when he tried on his own and slid deeper into the tub. Water sloshed, splashing her already wet clothes with warmth. She wanted to crawl in with him, bask in the luxury of heated water and hug his very alive body. Instead, she set the glass on the nearest shelf in the massive bathroom and then gave him her forearm as a non-slippery surface to help gain traction and hoist himself up.

"Toothbrush," he croaked. "Please."

"We already—"

He shook his head. "Please."

Shaking water from her fingers, Bella went to the sink and retrieved his toothbrush and the jar of mint powder for cleaning. After preparing the brush for him, she handed it over and waited while he cleaned his mouth. Again. He handed it back and then scrubbed soapy fingers through his beard. Again. Bella feared he'd never think he was clean enough to leave the tub. Lunah grumbled from her spot near the door on a plush cream rug.

The haze from soap obscured his nudity enough to keep Bella's cheeks from flaming anytime she looked his direction. He'd been too exhausted to notice her embarrassment. Not that she figured he had any. Sick or not, he was *very* comfortable in his skin. And a body like his? He had every right to be. Outside of art, the male form was, or rather had been, a mystery. All hard muscle, crisp hair, and so, *so* different from her, Bella had forced herself not to stare, many times, while assisting him out of his nasty clothes.

Washing him had led to completely inappropriate thoughts given the situation. She'd had to force her thoughts to remain focused on the reason her soapy hands had covered almost every inch of him. From between his toes to under his chin. Considering it a violation of his trust and privacy, she'd avoided his groin area, which he'd handled the moment he was strong enough, while she turned her back.

He disappeared under the water. Bella stepped forward, concerned, but he slowly rose, water sleuthing from his face and hair. He wiped his hand down his eyes and blinked droplets free.

"You need to drink more of the tea," Bella said.

"I will, after I get out."

She moved closer to the door. "I'll go get Nick."

"*Vye.*" He shook his head and sighed. "Please. I just... *vye.*"

Bella glanced into the decadent bedroom, complete with thick carpeting and a massive bed, that she swore was larger than her entire house, and pressed her lips together. "I can't carry you."

He grunted and braced his arms on the

edge of the tub. "I can walk." Her skepticism must have shown, for he laughed. "I can."

His laughter loosened something in her chest, and she had to turn away before she cried. "I'll get you something to wear."

"*Vye*, just a towel will be fine."

Bella changed direction and went to a wide shelving unit stocked full of plush towels. She plucked one free, resisting the urge to hug the softness and returned to the tub. Shaking it open, she held the fabric like a shield and focused on Lunah. Water sloshed and splashed. The towel pulled free from her fingers. He weaved on his feet and Bella reached to steady him. Solid muscle met her hand, slick and warm from the bath.

"Naked with a beautiful woman," he said, chuckling. "And me too weak to do anything useful about it."

Heat spread through Bella. "Probably for the best."

"I disagree," he whispered. His eyes, so close, were molten gold.

His name left her mouth on a plea.

He sighed and patted her hand. "I know. Help me to the bed."

Bella wrapped an arm around his back and accepted his weight. He clutched the towel to his groin but made no other effort to cover his nudity. One slow step at a time, they crossed to the bed.

"You should have let me get Nick," she said, his weight making her breathless.

"Nope. He's already seen me weak enough."

"Really?" Bella asked in disbelief. "This is a tough guy thing? Not wanting any help?"

"You're helping me."

"I'm not sure if this qualifies as help."

He fell onto the bed, and she yanked the blankets back while he scooted onto the wall of pillows against a thick mahogany headboard. He waited until she'd handed him the blankets to remove the towel. Eyes closed, he leaned back and relaxed. Lunah hopped onto the bed, wiggling her way to him, where she laid her head on his thighs and sighed in happiness.

The bond between her and the canine had faded into a warm ball of comfort. If Bella searched within herself, she could find the faint thread. At the end of which was a happy wolf. Lunah's two favorite people were occupying the same space, all was right in her world. Bella wasn't sure if Lunah controlled the strength of their connection or it was something she herself did. The moment they found Markus, the link had dimmed, and Lunah's voice had waned.

Bella retrieved the glass of tea and set it on the nightstand for when he awoke. He'd drifted into sleep and she didn't want to wake him. Tiptoeing across the room, she jumped when his voice cut the silence.

"Please don't leave," he said, his words fatigue heavy and deeper than normal.

Bella looked over her shoulder to find him watching her. "I can't stay in here."

He patted the blankets beside him. "*Dak,* you can. Right here. *Halrogva.* Please."

When she stayed where she was, he tried again. "I have much I have to tell you." She struggled to make sense of his words, his accent rougher than normal in his lethargy. "I don't want to have to try to find you when I wake up."

"You're naked," she blurted before she could stop herself.

"I'll control myself if you can," he said, his eyes drifting closed.

Control herself? While she could imagine exploring all the interesting aspects of his body, she didn't know the first thing about seduction, or even what a man liked or wanted. And yes, okay, she admitted, she definitely *wanted* to find out. With him. Not right now however, when he was unconscious and there was still a serious threat of him losing everything he'd managed to drink when he awoke. Eslainte had warned the drug would take time to leave his system and he wasn't free and clear of the nausea.

Sighing, she climbed onto the opulent mattress, her knees sinking into the bedding. Lunah gave her a cursory glance before returning her head to Markus's legs. Bella settled against the stacked pillows on her side and took hold of his hand, lacing their fingers together. He squeezed, but said nothing, his breathing evening in seconds.

Only the soft light of a single lamp burning near the door, and the fire from the hearth, filled the room. The curtains were closed against any intruding moonlight. Bella watched him sleep and dozed a few times, rousting when he moved, or moaned in discomfort, or woke long enough for her to convince him to take a sip or two.

When the pale glow of morning brightened the edges of the curtains, Lunah chuffed to get Bella's attention. She scooted off the bed and waited for the wolf to do the same. Casting a quick glance at Markus to make sure he'd slept through their movement, she went to the door. Lunah led the way downstairs and to the greenhouse, and then pawed at the glass door. Since Markus often left her to her own devices in the huge enclosed space, Bella figured she was safe to do the same.

A woman dressed in a dark blue uniform carried a tray up the stairs ahead of Bella. When the woman turned on the landing to head down the hall where Markus's room was located, Bella hurried her steps to follow. The staff member paused at Markus's door, shifting the tray to one hand as she reached for the door. Bella outright ran.

"I'll take that," she said, reaching for the tray.

"Oh, it's fine, I always bring him his breakfast," the woman said, a smile shining in her pretty hazel blue eyes.

"He's not feeling well." Bella tried to take the tray again, but the woman shifted away.

"It's my job, so if you could just—"

"You are *not* feeding him!" Bella growled, her outburst a shock even to herself.

The woman's eyes widened, and Bella realized, too late, she'd made a claim without any right. Before she could back away, slowly, and withdraw her statement, the attendant shoved the tray at Bella and rushed to the stairs. Squaring her shoulders, she opened the door, her hopes that Markus hadn't been awake to overhear her little lapse of sanity dashed. He stared at her, an amused smile toying at his lips.

"I'm glad you think it's funny," she snapped, closing the door with her foot. "She probably thinks I've lost my mind."

"Have you?" The blankets pooled at his waist, exposing his toned torso and the dark shadow of hair across his chest. The thought of the woman seeing him like *that* made an unpleasant emotion bloom in her chest.

"No. Yes. Maybe, I don't know. I didn't..." Bella took a deep breath. "I didn't like the idea of her bringing you food, which is weird."

Markus patted the mattress on the edge. "Come here."

Bella crossed the distance, handing him the tray before sitting. He set it off to the side, and then, much to her surprise, hauled her onto his lap. The plates and cup clattered on the tray, but nothing fell off or spilled.

Unsure what to do, and afraid to move, Bella braced her hands on his wide shoulders and stared into his eyes. "What are you doing?"

"We need to talk, and I don't want you going anywhere," he said, his arms wrapping around her hips.

"This isn't appropriate. If someone walks in..."

His eyes grew dark and his face lost all playfulness. "They'll see me with my mate."

Bella's heart stuttered. She tried to move off him, but he clamped his arms to her thighs and held her immobile.

"Correct me if I get any of this wrong, but I'm sure I wasn't imagining you say you could *hear* Lunah when you found me."

CHAPTER

TEN

Bella froze in his arms. Not a single muscle even twitched under his hold. Markus lifted a brow and waited. She licked her lips, and he made the mistake of looking at her perfect, very close, very tempting mouth. He was still naked under the blankets, which didn't provide near enough padding between their bodies for her to fail to notice his reaction if he didn't look away. Fast.

"Who took you?" she asked, changing the subject, which he'd anticipated.

"We'll get to that. First, answer my question."

Her fingers flexed on his shoulders. Tears filled her eyes as she looked away from him, her focus on the tray. "I'm so sorry."

"What for?"

"Nick told me if I bonded with Lunah, we could find you, but that by doing so, you'd never be able to bond with your chosen mate."

The words tumbled from her in a rush. "I didn't know what else to do, and Lunah—"

"Couldn't have bonded with you if we hadn't already established the link." He moved his hands to her thighs and squeezed until she met his stare. "I don't know when it happened exactly but I'd already bonded with you."

"Nick said that, too." She blinked, her eyelashes wet with unshed tears. "Why didn't you say anything?"

"And have you reject me?"

She looked away again. "Your country won't accept me."

"No, they won't. But that's not your problem."

"It shouldn't be yours, either," she whispered.

He knew he couldn't explain how important she was to him now. How their relationship took precedence over anything else for him. He brushed curls behind her ears and traced the gentle line of her jaw. "Bella, it's not a problem for me either. I don't care what anyone in Ruthenia thinks. I won't be living there, will I?"

She tried to move off him again, and again he held her in place. "You can't give up your home for me."

"I'm not giving up anything. I'm pretty sure, if you agree to a life with me, I'll be gaining much more."

A tear spilled down her cheek. Markus sat up while pressing into her low back to shift her closer. He brushed his lips to hers, careful to keep the kiss chaste. For now. "Do you agree to being my mate?" he asked against her lips.

She laughed out a sob, her breath fluttering across his mouth. She sat back enough to meet his gaze, her fingers feathering across his mouth in a trembling touch. "Are you sure?"

"Never been more certain in my life," he answered, no hesitation, and kissed her fingertips.

"I feel like I should be asking you that question."

"Then ask."

She laughed again, another tear racing down her cheek, making her ocean green eyes bright even in the shadowy room. "Markus," her voice waivered and she took a deep breath and continued, "yes, I will be your mate, if you'll be mine."

"*Dak.*"

She didn't give him the chance to celebrate his enormous win with another, deeper kiss. "Who took you?"

"Adelaine and her lover, Flynn."

Bella wrinkled her nose. "Flynn is her lover? Isn't he a lot younger than her?"

"Probably by thirty years, if not more."

A shudder ran through her.

"Yeah, it was pretty awful having to listen to them."

"They..."

"*Dak.*"

She hugged him, her whole body wrapped around him. "I'm so sorry."

"I'll get all the information together and bring it to Shield Guardian Perrella. She's already plotted her next murder. One of her younger singers, she plans to kill her in winter and hide her body in the snow, like she froze to death walking to a corner store or something. We can't let that happen."

Bella released her hold and sat back. "Without more evidence of the other crimes, I'm not sure what he can do."

"If he looks at all the murders as a whole, I think he'll agree, the *accidental* aspect becomes lost when all the women were, at one time, her pupils, and all of them died by means made to appear chance. The peanut one is especially suspect after learning the other facts," Markus said.

Her eyes widened. "You learned something, before they took you."

Markus nodded. "Adelaine was indeed the voice teacher to all the deceased singers. I was even able to speak with two families over the radio who don't reside here in Sziveria. They'd sent their daughters to be tutored by Adelaine. One a decade ago, another around eighteen years." He tapped his temple. "They took my notebook after they abducted me, but I remember what the families told me. Perrella can conduct his own interviews with my information."

"I agree, I hope he does, too."

"I have no authority in Sziveria, but I heard her confession when she kidnapped me, and will write my statement. If they choose not to do anything about her, the next death is on them."

"What about your capture?" she asked.

Markus shook his head. "I can't have anyone learn how to weaken me. I don't know how she found out."

Bella touched his cheek and he pressed into her caress. "What did she give you?"

"I don't know, some sort of sedative. Ruthenian's are sensitive to most pain reducers and sedatives. It's not unknown for a regular dose for most people to be fatal for us."

Color faded from Bella's cheeks. "She wanted to kill you."

"*Dak*, that was her intent."

Her hand dropped and she hugged herself. "If I hadn't bonded to Lunah, you would have died."

Gently, Markus pried her left arm free and brush the bandage wrapped around her forearm and down the thick leather bracer she still wore, still damp from helping him in the tub. "You may not have wanted to admit it yet, but I was yours to save."

Before she could argue, Markus sat up and locked his mouth over hers. He'd almost died. Almost lost the chance to taste her again. To feel her body, warm and supple under his hands. And while he wanted more, wanted everything, he knew despite their mated status, she needed that contract with his signature. Markus respected her culture even as she licked her way into his mouth.

The covers weren't thick enough to hide his desire. Not that Bella seemed to mind. A little moan vibrated into his mouth and she rocked, sending pleasurable fire through his veins. Markus slid his hands under her shirt and dug his fingers into the flesh of her hips. Little sparks nipped at his fingertips. The smooth heat of her skin teased his senses.

"*Krahet'sna,* you are a temptation to me," he whispered against her wet mouth.

She trailed her lips along his bearded jaw to his neck, where she nipped and breathed his scent in deep. Markus shuddered and dropped his head back.

"What does that mean?" she asked.

Markus stared at the ceiling, trying to understand her words, his body taunt with need. "What?"

She continued on her quest, her tongue leaving a scalding trail to his collarbone. "The word you said, kra something, what does it mean?"

"*Krahet'sna,*" he repeated. "Beautiful."

She sat back and stared at him. Markus slid his hands up her smooth back to her shoulder blades and pressed her closer, kissing her.

"That's what you are to me. Beautiful," he said.

Her eyes shone. In feathery touches, she

traced his nose, cheeks and eyebrows. "You are that to me, too."

Markus kissed her again. Deeper. Longer. His passion a fiery knot in his chest. He hugged her. Moaning, she wrapped her arms around his shoulders, her fingers tangling into his long, unbound hair. Inside her mouth, his tongue explored and teased. Desperate to feel more of her, Markus slipped a hand between them and found her breast. She gasped into his mouth and inched far enough back to allow him access. At last, he'd discover what she felt like in his palm. Her pebbled nipple brushed the center of his hand and he toyed with the sensitive nub.

She arched into his touch, encouraging him, letting him know without words she enjoyed the attention. Still, he wanted more. "Do you like that?" he breathed into her mouth.

She nodded, her fingers tightening in his hair.

Mindful of her lack of experience, he carefully took her nipple between his fingers and gently tweaked. "That?"

Her hips rocked again. Another nod.

Growling, Markus sat back and yanked her shirt up. Just as he'd imagined so many months ago, she was perfection. Small, round globes, big enough to feast on beckoned. He latched his mouth onto her breast. She cried out, holding his head as he sucked and laved. Pressure built low in his gut.

A heavy knock tore through their moment.

Markus released her breast and lifted his head, looking over her shoulder. Bella froze, her breath puffing across his ear. She tried to move off him, but he held her in place, letting her shirt fall.

"What?" he growled.

"I was just checking to make sure you're alive," Nick's muffled voice called through the door.

Markus shifted Bella across his erection. She trembled in his arms. "I'm very much alive, my friend."

"Okay, good. Let me know if you need anything else."

When Bella tried to move off him again, he released his hold and let her topple over. She fell onto her back and covered her eyes with her arm. "That was..."

Markus traced the smooth skin of her exposed stomach. "Something I wish we had more time to explore."

A tremor raced the length of her body. Her knees pressed together, making him smile.

Markus leaned over and kissed her cheek. Fluttering his touch along her ribcage, he found her breast under her shirt. "Contract with me."

Bella turned her head and met his gaze. "Yes."

THE THICK SCENT of earth hung in the warm, moist air. Bella looked around the greenhouse lobby in amazement. Saplings of dwarf oak, ash and red maples lined a path that wound through a spacious area at least three stories in height. The glass enclosure allowed sun to bleed in and heat the air. Even when snow collected in drifts outside, this green space would give residents a nature sanctuary. In the years to come, the infant trees would stretch to fill the space above with a lush canopy of green.

"What are we doing here?" she asked, following behind Markus and Lunah.

"I have something to show you."

"How did the meeting with Shield Guardian Perrella go?" she asked, walking faster to catch up to him.

He shrugged and held open a door to a wide, switchback style staircase. The number one was painted in a big white digit on the wall beside the door. "Fine."

Bella grabbed his sleeve before he could set foot on the first stair. "I haven't seen you for two days because you were at the SNID, and it went *fine*?"

A quick yank pulled his arm free from her grasp and he started up the stairs after Lunah. "I wanted you there. But Perrella insisted his two leaders be present and I knew you'd rather not deal with the witch and the coward."

Bella laughed under her breath. "The coward?"

"Avner."

Her boots clomped on the wooden stairs. Lunah's nails scratched to catch the surface.

Markus made barely a whisper of sound. "I'm sure they weren't pleased to once again be shown evidence of a crime right under their noses."

"No, they weren't. This time at least it wasn't one of their cases or even something that had their attention."

"And they took it seriously? The evidence and the crimes?" she asked, holding onto the banister.

"Yes, they did." He turned at a switch back and kept going. "From my understanding, they were going to gather all the evidence, interview the families, and hoped to level accusations against Adelaine by the end of the week."

Bella glanced at the wall and noted the white three painted next to a door. She looked up, trying to judge how many floors the building had. "That soon?"

"They had almost everything they need. Once they speak to Miss Henley and verify the evidence still at the Vanscoyn residence, I'm positive they'll be able to move forward without any concerns."

"Was Banks satisfied with your answers?" she asked, her fingers trailing the cool wooden rail.

"He was, though I think knowing their daughter was murdered by someone they trusted was worse for his wife to learn. It's tragic, the entire situation."

Another floor passed her by, and she looked up, relieved to note they only had one more to go to the top. Markus's braid swung against his back, reminding her of the silken feel of the unbound strands. Heat blossomed in her cheeks. She'd spent the last two days in a state of distraction. At night, the sensation of his mouth on her skin filled her dreams and left her throbbing in need. Trailing behind him through the building was the first moment they'd had together since she left Nick's. She'd expected a kiss. A hug. Maybe even a squeeze of her hand. Instead, he ushered her into the building without a word.

Was he having second thoughts?

Not that she'd blame him if he did. And she was too big of a coward to ask. He held the door open to the fifth floor and Bella entered a luxurious hall. She paused, taking in the thick runner down a lengthy hall. There were only four doors, meaning the spaces beyond were huge.

"What is this place?" she asked.

"Come on." He took her hand, and once she started moving, he released her.

Bella frowned and rubbed her palms on her pants legs. An ache of worry settled in her chest. He stopped at the second door on the left. At an angle, the entrance was recessed enough to give the illusion of privacy. The knob opened without a key, though she noted he had one ready if necessary. Lunah's tail wagged a happy dance as she trotted past Markus inside.

Unsure of what awaited her, Bella slipped

by Markus. A vast, incomplete apartment greeted her. An entire wall of windows flooded the open space. Framework allowed her to get some sort of idea of what the home would look like one day. Only a single wall was complete, sectioning off into a hallway of some sort to her right. The scent of fresh wood filled the air. Behind her, the door clicked shut. Markus's strong arms slid around her waist and his chin rested on top of her head.

"Welcome home," he whispered.

Stunned, Bella stared. "What?"

"I bought this apartment. We're one of the first tenets. But, it can't be left unoccupied and they've assured me it'll be finished before Wintervial. Since you'll be my wife, I was hoping you'd live in our home until I returned after winter, at which point we'll live here. Together," he said.

Bella twisted in his arms. "Why did you do this?"

"Didn't you agree to be my wife?" His brows raised in question.

"Yes, I did."

"And did you think you'd still live in that hovel of a home while I'm away and unable to protect you?"

Actually, she had. "We haven't needed protection for the last three years. I think we'd be okay for four to six months."

He squeezed her to him. "I can't be in another country worrying about you."

Bella pushed away from him and faced the

unfinished construction. Insecure, she hugged herself. "This is too much."

Markus grabbed her hand and tugged her to the left. "Actually, it's just the right size. Let me show you."

Expressing an excitement she'd never seen in him before, he showed her four future bedrooms, the largest of which would belong to her mother. Too overwhelmed to say anything she allowed herself to be guided from one area to the next. Still holding her hand, he pulled her to the dining area and kitchen, separated from what would a spacious living room by generous arches that would allow the light from the floor-to-ceiling windows to reach through. He took her down the half-finished hall that would house a future office space and have a radio installed. The expense of that alone had made her choke.

"And this," he said, sweeping his arm in an arc, "will be our bedroom."

Her hand slid free of his. She wandered to a set of double glass doors leading out into a small balcony greenhouse. The windows of the greenhouse were removable for the more temperate summer months, allowing fresh air into their private room if they wanted. Bella closed her eyes and imagined a summer breeze cooling their damp skin after a night spent in each other's arms. *Yes.* She wanted that, so much.

"Are you nervous?" he asked behind her.

The view from five-stories captivated her.

Below, the pulse of the city threaded along the road, heading to and from Extilis Square. He'd bought an apartment in a coveted complex within walking distance to the most popular shopping destination in the city. Bella swallowed. She was out of her league here.

"About what?"

"Us. I know this is soon, but we'll live here for a very long time." He slipped his hands along her shoulders and turned her to face him.

"Markus," she began, unable to meet his stare, scared to know the answer to the question burning in her mind. "Are you sure, absolutely certain this what you want?"

"I have the contract ready. I leave tomorrow, and I'm hoping you'll sign it before I depart."

Bella's heart clenched. "We won't have any time together."

"I know, and I'm sorry for that. I'd like to wait, but I know you won't live here if you aren't my wife. Will you sign it? Please."

No words of love, or even of how much she meant to him. He wanted her safe. And she was too afraid to say the words without knowing if he felt the same. Not yet. She swallowed and nodded, not trusting her voice.

He kissed her. A gentle, sweet, press of his mouth to hers. "Thank you."

She couldn't help but laugh against his lips. "You bought me an apartment. What else would I say?"

"No?"

She wrapped her arms around him. "I agreed to marry you. Maybe this is sooner than I'd thought, but you're leaving, and I'm your mate, which isn't recognized in my country without the paper. Of course, I will sign it."

His gaze searched hers, sparking with golden fire. "My sons will have your eyes."

Smiling, she touched his bearded jaw. "And my daughters will have yours."

EPILOGUE

One month later...

A NEWSPAPER LANDED in front of Bella as she stirred honey into her tea. Madeleine tapped her finger under a heading. Leaning forward, Bella read over the article. "Wow, the accusation made the front page."

"Did you expect anything less?" her mother asked, sitting down at the table, a plate filled with toast, fried ham, and cut fruit in her hand. "I do believe this is the second serial killer your husband has helped rid our country of. Kind of terrifying if you ask me, to know we had two lurking about."

Bella frowned and pushed the paper away. Early morning sun glinted off her wedding band. "There are more than two, I'm afraid. Always will be."

Madeleine perched her fork over the food. "Well, I don't want to know about the rest." She paused with a bite halfway to her mouth. "At least, not until they've been caught."

Bella looked around their new home. Still amazed they lived in the opulent dwelling. Their lack of furniture was embarrassing, but she refused to purchase anything additional until Markus arrived back in Sziveria to help her choose. He did have a huge bed delivered for their room, which she found she couldn't sleep in. Not without him. The first night she'd tried, she'd felt too alone and had crawled into her tiny bed in one of the spare bedrooms. She knew she'd adjust, but so far, the bed was just a bed, it wasn't their bed yet.

Closing her eyes, she swallowed against the pain of missing him. As if he'd sensed her melancholy from hundreds of miles away, the radio chirped an incoming call. Madeleine laughed as Bella jumped from her chair and raced to the office. She snatched the receiver off the large transmitter.

"Hello?"

His deep voice cracked across the line, making her heart expand with joy. "Hello, *Kra-het'sna.*"